SQUABBLE
AND OTHER STORIES

SQUABBLE

AND OTHER STORIES

John Holman

TICKNOR & FIELDS
NEW YORK 1990

For my family and friends

For information about permission to reproduce selections from
this book, write to Permissions, Ticknor & Fields, 215 Park
Avenue South, New York, New York 10003.

Library of Congress Cataloging-in-Publication Data

Holman, John, date.
  Squabble and other stories / John Holman.
      p.   cm.
  ISBN 0-89919-935-6
  I. Title.
PS3558.035593S65   1990   89-20498
813'.54 — dc20   CIP

Printed in the United States of America

BP 10 9 8 7 6 5 4 3 2 1

Some of the stories in this book first appeared in the following
publications: *The New Yorker, The Crescent Review, Epos, The
Mississippi Review, Carolina Quarterly,* and *Fiction Quarterly
(Tampa Tribune).*

This work was supported, in part, by the University of South
Florida Research and Creative Scholarship Grant Program
under Grant No. 1104 934 RO.

Contents

SQUABBLE

Aaron thought about retrenchment. That was what the dean had termed it, peppering his letter with other such phrases — "financial cutbacks" and "organizational shifts." If the dean had simply written "Last hired, first fired," Aaron would not have needed an extra few seconds to catch the drift.

Anyway, he was back in his hometown, living with his aunt — no hope of teaching in the fall and no desire to move again, either. He had watched the late-night Employment Security Commission report on TV and heard of an opening for an electrical engineer with twenty years' experience. He had a Ph.D. in geography. His morning mail included a job list bearing a yellow sticker with his change of address and listing nothing he was qualified for.

As he sat in his pajamas on the porch, the late May sun across his lap, a Skylark pulled into the driveway, the

exhaust clean and guttural. Aaron had watched the spar-
kling old white convertible roar up and down the street
several times that morning, its red roof puffed with wind.
Dennis, his buddy from high school, whom he had seen
maybe twice in seven years of grad school and teaching,
leaped out of the car, wearing cutoff khakis and black-
and-red high-top basketball shoes. His sweatshirt was inside out and the sleeves were cut away. He carried a Wil-
son basketball and a yellow thermos.

"I'm a foreman at the factory, I still play a little ball,
and I frequent a dive," Dennis said when Aaron asked
what he had been up to.

"The car, those shoes," Aaron said.

"Gotta keep up with the jitterbugs, since I can't keep up
with the Joneses," Dennis said, and he slapped Aaron's
knee with the palmed ball.

"I need a job."

"So get one."

They drank Dennis's Kickapoo juice, a mild mix of
orange juice and gin, from clear plastic cups Aaron
brought out.

"There's a guy at this dive you gotta see," Dennis said.
"He's Clara's nephew. It's Clara's new place. He's got half
a face from prison surgery."

"What does he do?"

"He's the life of the party."

Aaron thought a place that prized a half-a-face ex-con
would be a good place to work. He could tend bar, just
pour shots and open beers. Maybe not even open them. "I
want to work at the dive," he said.

"Well, clean up. We'll talk to Clara. You seen her yet?"

"Not yet. You talk to her first. I haven't kept contact."

"I know."

After Dennis left, Aaron took a shower and put on fresh clothes — white deep-pleated cuffed pants and a checked blue shirt. He slipped on last summer's espadrilles, got the car keys his aunt had left before she flew away on vacation, and drove into town in her new blue Topaz.

The skyline was changing. Places were sprouting all over. Streets were barricaded, sidewalks torn up. He parked on a side street and walked inside the new Tower Plaza. He decided the Tower must be a city project. An entrepreneur would have piped in some music. It was pristinely quiet, not many people. Otherwise, things looked nice. A wide circular stairway went up a few levels. On the entrance level there were mostly cafés — China Falls, Indian Cuisine, Mexican Pleasure, Victoria's Jubilee.

He went inside Mexican Pleasure and sat at the bar. The motif was Art Deco Mexican — shiny surfaces and large sharp angles. There was low-volume Trini Lopez music from some unseen speakers. The woman behind the bar looked bored. She didn't look Mexican. Doughy and young, in a white off-the-shoulder blouse and colorful striped skirt, she seemed embarrassed to be wearing a costume.

"Where is everybody?" Aaron asked.

"This time of day is dead," she said. "Our special today is gin and tonic."

Aaron asked for a beer and lit a cigarette. "Is that music your choice or the management's?"

"I could change it. Pay up first."

He did, and she went out through a swinging door behind the bar. When she returned, some piano jazz started playing. Then another woman came through the door with a glass of iced tea. Aaron smiled at her. She was wearing the same getup as the bartender, and her hair was bright blond, pulled tight into a ponytail. She came around the bar and sat two stools away.

"I got some lousy tips," she said to the bartender, spreading bills and coins on the bar top. "Ten dollars and a Canadian nigger."

Aaron looked over at her, and at the first woman. Neither looked at him. Maybe he had heard wrong.

A tall black woman peeped in the entrance, lingered a little to look at Aaron, and went away. The woman with the tips started talking about Mr. T. She was talking about his haircut.

"What do you think?" She was speaking to Aaron. "I could do with a style, am I right?"

He smiled again. He still had his beer to finish, which was dark, imported, and good. He drank it rather fast anyway. He left the bartender a hefty tip.

He saw the tall black woman browsing in a jewelry store where an Oriental man sat behind a low glass counter stringing gold-bead necklaces. The woman's feet were spread ducklike. He walked up beside her and stood on the plum carpet. Fluorescent lights were overhead and in all the counters. The jeweler had a glass to his eye, and his face was tinged blue from the long piece of blue felt cushioning the gold.

"This stuff is all broken," Aaron said to the woman. She was young, maybe twenty-one at most. "You don't want this stuff."

"Jeepers, you're right. I don't want this stuff."

She looked at him. Her eyes were as brown as bottles and seemed the same color as her skin. He unrolled his shirt sleeve, buttoned the cuff, and started on the other one.

"I don't want anything," she said, as if just that moment realizing it.

"Then you don't mind if I stay?"

"Why should I?" She walked out.

Aaron caught up with her at China Falls. It was a takeout place with orange neon trimming the order window. She stood talking through the window. Her hair was long, loose, and dry-looking. Her jeans were tight, and she wore a big white T-shirt.

"That was a nasty trick," Aaron said. "I'm devastated."

"That reminds me of a song."

"You're not supposed to find fault."

"O.K. I feel sorry for you. What's your name?"

"Aaron. You can be Caroline."

"I'll stick with Wanda," she said. "You be Taiwo."

"No. I be Aaron."

Her egg-drop soup came to the window in a clear plastic bowl with a beige plastic spoon. Wanda took it to an iron table, and Aaron brought over a few napkins.

"This is delicious," she said.

"It looks nutritious."

She swirled the soup with a spoon. "Want some?"

He shook his head. "Is this a good place? I was just insulted back there in the Mexican place. Racial stuff."

"Really? Never happened to me. I don't have time for it."

"I guess I do."

"It's the town. Neo-hick."

"I was born here. Where are you from?"

"Nowhere. Notice an accent? I go to school. Sing and dance and say the words. I'm decultured by culture. I'm an actress."

"That's nice. How do I look?"

"Spiffy."

"Thanks. That's what I was shooting for. It's important when you're between jobs."

"I guess." She dabbed her mouth with a napkin. "What jobs are you between?"

"Geography teacher and bartender. My interview is tonight. I'd invite you if you wanted."

"Invite me anyway." She tilted the bowl and poured the last of the soup onto the spoon.

That night, Aaron stood at the end of the driveway waiting for Wanda, not wanting her to miss the house. It was set back from the road behind eighty-year-old trees. He had been waiting twenty minutes, since dusk. Fireflies were out. He wore black — silk shirt, pleated pants, shiny loafers. Neo-hick, he thought. She pulled into the driveway in an orange Chevette. He had made a pitcher of grape Kool-Aid and placed it and two glasses on a TV tray on the porch. He had lit a low flame in a hurricane lamp. Wanda wore a denim miniskirt and a beaded African bracelet, perfume, a purple T-shirt, a matador's jacket, and purple sandals. Her hair was combed a little wilder.

"You always look so city," Aaron said.

"You live in the sticks, man. Took me forever."

"We call it the country."

"Sure you do." She looked him over. "Wyatt Earp?"

"I'm still real. What about you?"

"Don't I act like it?"

He led her up the steps to a lawn chair and poured the Kool-Aid. He took a chair on the other side of the tray.

"Mind if I smoke?" he said. "I ask because you look so healthy." He lit the cigarette and fanned periodically to keep the smoke from lingering too long between them.

"Do you think I'll get the job?"

"There's probably no doubt about it. What's this bar like?"

"It's called the Bellaire. I've never been. Started up while I was away. It's sort of illegal."

"Don't get me arrested," she said. "Who's the clientele?"

"People with no time for racial stuff. You ought to fit in."

"Gee whiz, man. Don't be so cute."

"Gee whiz? What language are we speaking?"

"Squabble. We're squabbling."

"You can get along, can't you?"

"I'm here. Squabbling's good now and then."

"Kiss me."

"You kiss me."

They stared at each other.

"Why don't I just take these things inside."

He stood the tray by the kitchen sink. He ran water over the cigarette and put it in the garbage. He came back, pulled the door, and blew out the lamp. Wanda stood with her back to him, looking out toward the fireflies, hips and shoulders as sturdy as a statue's.

"I'll drive," she said. "You're nervous."

"Fine," he said, glad she wanted to drive. The interview was half a joke anyway. He wasn't sure what Wanda thought he was nervous about.

Clara had told him that afternoon he could work anytime he wanted. It was after meeting Wanda at the Tower that he'd driven out June Street, a pitted rock road shaped like a *b,* sided by dusty woods that gave way to small frame houses like his, separated by wide yards. Dennis's Skylark was in Clara's driveway, and Dennis and a fat man were sitting in the yard by Clara's tan brick house, on metal and wood auditorium chairs. The yard was landscaped with winter-killed shrubs and blue ceramic chickens. The fat man was dark and shirtless, with the legs of his pants rolled to the knees and one foot submerged in a tin pail of water. He fanned himself with a large elephant-ear leaf from a weed that grew unchecked and fuzzy against the side of the house. He looked extremely hot and agitated.

Dennis introduced Aaron as Dr. Stets. "This is Duke," he said of the fat man. "Clara's boyfriend."

Duke shook hands weakly. "Take a look at these feet, Doc," he said. "They're killing me."

The foot resting on the short brown grass was so swollen that the yellowed nails were nearly buried in flesh.

"I'm not that kind of doctor," Aaron said. "But you ought to see one."

Duke looked disgusted and waved the fuzzy leaf at him.

"Let's go inside," Dennis said. "Clara would love to see you."

Clara's screen door was decorated with aluminum birds. Dennis led the way into a darkened living room with low fifties furniture covered in puckered plastic. It was years since Aaron had been here. They went through a doorless entrance to the kitchen, where Clara stood at the sink drying dishes.

"Look who's back," Dennis said.

Clara turned around, smiled broadly, and said, "Well, if it ain't the good doctor. I'm not too well today. Can you get me a private room?"

"I'm not that kind of doctor, Clara."

"Oh? What kind are you?"

"Just a different kind."

She walked over, sliding her feet in scuffed men's leather slippers, and hugged him. She was wide and soft, and her cheek was wet. She smelled of baby powder. She moved to an oscillating fan on the counter, put her face down to the grille, and then turned around to let it blow on her back. "Air conditioner's broke. Over there is Claude, my nephew you never met."

Claude, hard-looking and lean, sat in a breakfast nook. Aaron had to step farther into the kitchen to see him, sitting at a Formica table eating a bowl of navy beans.

"Dog," he said. "Call me Dog."

Dennis snickered and made a face of mock fright. Dog's right cheekbone was gone and replaced with a long slick scar. "I'm as drunk as a skunk," Dog said. "Beans?" he offered, without looking up or altering his hunched posture over the bowl.

Squeezed into Wanda's Chevette, smelling her light perfume, Aaron considered that bringing her to the Bellaire was not a good idea. June Street was bumpy and dark, with only lights in back windows to mark the houses. Seeing it as she must, he thought it looked like another planet. He had told Dennis, using the language of high school, that Wanda was a first-round draft choice, no tryout necessary, so he had to back it up. But he didn't want to scare her.

The Bellaire was at the bottom of the *b*. A few cars were pulled into the yard. Dennis's Skylark was on the roadside, and Aaron pointed for Wanda to park by it. Three gray plank steps led to a small gray deck where Duke, dressed in a burgundy short-sleeved shirt, dark pants, and black socks on his swollen feet, leaned over the rail. He'd had his hair done up in tight, oily curls.

"Evening, Duke," Aaron said.

Duke straightened up and said to Wanda, "Ma'am, you have to leave your purse outside unless you want me to search it. You can leave your some-kind-of-doctor out, too, unless you want me to search him."

Wanda went back to the car. When she opened the trunk, a light came on and Aaron could see the taut mus-

cles of her thigh as she bent to place the purse under
something. The gold of her jacket glittered. Then Duke's
hands started moving over Aaron's ribs and down his legs.
"Anything in the socks?"

Aaron lifted his pants to show he wasn't wearing any.
"What's this about?"

"Trouble. Don't want none." He snorted.

Wanda came back and flashed a game smile. "She's
clean," Aaron said, gangster-style, and Duke let them
through.

Inside was a living room with card tables and straight-
backed chairs instead of regular living room furniture,
arranged on a scuffed hardwood floor. The room was long,
and maybe some walls had been knocked down to make
the bedrooms part of the action. A raised plywood dance
floor was at the rear, with a jukebox booming out funk
tunes. A bar was just to the left, where Dennis and Dog
sat drinking from Dixie cups. When Dennis saw them, he
stood and waved his hand at some empty stools. They sat,
and Aaron introduced Wanda.

"Nice," she said, and looked up to scan the walls. Signs,
hand-painted in red, were everywhere — house codes of
behavior: "NO CURSING," "NO DRINKING OR SMOKING ON THE
DANCE FLOOR," "CASH ONLY," "IF YOU ARE JEALOUS OF YOUR
MAN OR WOMAN GO HOME." Another sign, propped against
the wall behind a cardboard box, read:

"NEW YEAR'S EVE
DANCING HATS."

"So chic," Dog said.

Aaron nudged Wanda, who had shifted her gaze to the

people around the room. There weren't many. It was early. Dog repeated the compliment.

"Holy moly," Wanda said. "What happened to your face?"

"So brave, too. I'm attracted to temerity. Dance with me and I'll tell you."

They left, linking fingers, for the dance floor. Clara was sitting behind the bar near the computerized cash register, and Aaron asked her for two beers. She rolled back the stainless steel top of a gas station cooler and took out two tall Millers. She wore a black-and-gold cycling cap and a lime green cardigan over a white diner uniform. The air conditioning worked here. In the smoky light from a lectern lamp mounted on the register, her face pocketed shadows, like dented metal.

Aaron turned toward her on his stool. "Are you sure you ought to be here? You don't look well."

"That line's not too popular," she said, and then let out a loud, long laugh.

"She's on medication," Dennis said. "Now, Wanda, I can tell, is drug-free. Never had an aspirin. Look at her slam-dunking Dog."

Aaron slid around. Wanda and Dog had cleared out a space for themselves. The other dancers had about lost their rhythm as they watched Dog doing a silly knee dance and Wanda showing off her art school energy. She was all movement, muscles and hair, circles and angles, reaching down low and pulling something unseen from the red-and-blue air, reaching up and pulling something else, spinning and shaking something to death with her teeth. Dog was nearly applauding, splashing his Dixie cup empty.

"He's as happy as a sissy at the Y," Clara said, letting loose that laugh again.

On her way back to the bar, Wanda turned down two drunks who met her crouched in knee-bent dance postures, snapping their fingers. Dog sat again beside Dennis, Wanda beside Aaron.

Dog pulled his shirt cuffs so they showed out the sleeves of his shiny blue jacket. "She's perfect," he said.

Aaron thought Dog didn't look too bad all dressed up. His suit was impossibly blue. His face was playful, with a friendly smile that might have been infectious if it could spread to more right cheek. Wanda gave Dog a seated bow and sipped from her can of beer. Clara moved off her chair behind the cash register and brought Wanda a cup.

"Thanks," Wanda said.

"You want a job? I'd pay you to come in and dance like that, keep my customers coming in and thirsty."

"That's my job," Dog said.

Wanda waved her hands. "No, thanks. This guy's the one who needs work."

"He's overqualified and can't do nothing no way," Clara said. "But his momma and daddy were friends of mine. His daddy died in Korea, you know. And she bled to death when he was a baby. His aunt don't like me, though. She raised him after his folks died. Moved all the way from Jersey to raise him. He tell you that? I don't want no trouble with her. I'm his momma, too, but he don't act like it. Hell, I don't act like it."

Wanda had one leg crossed over the other, and one finger, just one long glossed fingernail, between her teeth. She had been frowning since his parents were mentioned.

"I just met the guy," she said. They both looked at Aaron.

"I guess he can open some beers and pour straight," Clara said.

Aaron went around to where part of the bar top lifted up, and got behind. He rolled up his sleeves and the cooler top, flexed his fingers, and started opening cans and bottles really fast. When he finished, his silk sleeves hung loose and beers were lined up, some foaming over. His fingers hurt. Dennis and Wanda applauded him slowly.

"Not bad," Clara said. "All you need now is some customers and some sleeve garters."

Aaron shouted, "Anybody want a beer?"

A few people at nearby tables looked but didn't get up. One man kept his head down on his folded arms. Those dancing kept dancing. Wanda raised her hand, and Aaron gave her one. He pushed the rest toward Dennis and Dog.

"Watch out," Dog said. "My dates are here." Two young women were standing by the door. "They drink like Maseratis."

The women were unsmiling. They approximated Wanda's style — short skirts, T-shirts — but with high heels and lacy anklets. Their skirts were leather, one black and one red, and they were heavily into makeup and frosted hair.

Dog introduced them with a flourish: "Ebony Angel and Pinky." He gave each a beer. Aaron took the money from the bills on the bar in front of Dog.

"Let's get a table," Dog said. "Take a break," he said to Aaron.

Dennis pulled two card tables together and Aaron joined them, bringing the rest of the opened beers.

"What's with the search?" Ebony Angel asked. She was gold-skinned, with buzzed temples and a yellow fringe of hair at the top. She looked to Aaron like Woodstock the bird, except her eye shadow was rainbows.

"We had a fellow get shotgunned last week," Dog said.

"Googly moogly," Wanda said.

"You believe that?" Pinky, heavier and darker than Ebony Angel, looked at Wanda incredulously. "I don't believe *you*."

"Right over there," Dog said, pointing at the door. "Maybe it was last month. Two fellows sitting on those stools started fussing at the bar. Somebody's mother was mentioned. Another fellow, tired of hearing it, said he had a shotgun in his car. He threw his keys on the bar and one of them picked them up, got the gun, came back, and shot. The poor fellow was on his way out."

Dog sat back looking smug, as if no one could challenge him. They all looked at him and kept quiet for a while.

"Guess how old I am," Dog said. "Fifty-five. You believe that?"

"Why not?" Pinky said. She had pink metallic lips. She pressed them together and relaxed them full again, like an instant azalea blossom.

"Are you always so beautiful?" Wanda said.

"Every day. We both are."

"They're sex muffins," Dog said.

"No, we are not. We are women," Pinky said.

Dog put his nose to Ebony Angel's neck. She laughed and pushed him away with her hand on his forehead.

"You smell like muffins."

"We don't even like sex," Ebony Angel said.

Dennis, looking at Aaron, mouthed the words, "You believe that?"

Aaron shrugged.

"I don't care," Dog said. "I am glad to be alive. Glad to be out. I went to prison innocent, right? Fifteen years. All I did was give a fellow a ride. Said he wanted bubble gum and robbed the damn store. So they said I had cancer and they whittled my face. Really, I look better. Kept me out of trouble, that's a fact. Now I'm back among family and the free. When I was in the joint, I read *Time* magazine the whole time. Y'all don't surprise me a bit."

"Say something in *Time*," Dennis said.

"I only know a few words."

"I know *Time*," Wanda said. "Salubrious, dolorous, specious."

"You don't know squat," Pinky said.

"I know your daddy."

"I've got a shotgun in the car," Dennis said.

"So do I," Pinky said.

"Great," Wanda said. "Let's get dangerous."

"Let's dance," Dennis said to Pinky.

Dog and Ebony Angel got up, too.

"That was cute," Aaron said.

"That was squabble." Wanda winked.

Another couple came in and took seats at the bar. They wore matching yellow suits and caps.

"Shouldn't you be helping?" Wanda asked.

"Possibly."

"I might dance some more. Get to know your friends."

"They're not my friends, except Dennis."

"They're friendly, though."

"Somewhat."

"You should see me perform. I'm slow in real life. Not like Dog's dates."

"I don't know. I can't keep up with you."

"Good. That means I'm winning."

"Winning what?"

"You know. The game, the race, the war." She took off her jacket and draped it on the back of the chair. "You really do need a new name," she said. "From now on you are Nick. You're a tough guy. Get yourself a hat, too."

"You're sweet," he said.

"Sure I am. I'm molasses." She smacked her lips.

"You know what I'm thinking?" Aaron said. "I'm thinking I've got to fall in love with you. I'm thinking it's urgent. Otherwise Pinky or Ebony Angel is gonna make me marry her and take out her future on me. But this is a struggle, because quite frankly I'm losing the will to get to know you."

She held out her hands, palms up. "No problem, Nick," she said, and laughed. "Know what I mean?"

"Right," he said. "Give me a clue. Are we squabbling?"

She clasped her hands behind her head. "I don't squabble with Nick."

He gave her the O.K. sign. He got up and went behind the bar. Clara tied a butcher's apron around him, and he nodded to the couple in yellow. Each smoked an extra-long cigarette, and they seemed to be sharing a wine cooler. Duke hobbled in, jiggling flesh, and eased his weight onto a stool. He lifted a foot over the opposite knee and pulled at the elastic sock. Aaron asked what he could get him, but he said he didn't drink. "Real doctor's orders."

So Aaron looked at Wanda, who was watching him, moving her head to the music. She was beautiful, having the time of her life, he supposed. He thought he should go back over there and kiss her. He figured it needed doing. But first he would check out the stock behind the bar, just to get his bearings, before the all-night crowd rushed in.

PESO STREET

Ted sat in the sweltering den of a second-floor apartment in an old brick building on Peso Street. He sipped his piña colada, glanced at the moist faces of the men around the small oval table, and chuckled about the rubber fish that the man to his left kept next to his beer. The man rubbed it. "For luck," he said, and he placed a three of clubs on the table. There was a knock on the front door. Ted studied his hand and played a low diamond. Then strangers stood at the door of the den.

The woman wore a soft white dress with a lace boat-neck collar and a long, lace border at the hem. Her hair was straight and braided in the back around two blue silk flowers. After a moment, Ted recognized Paul, the man in the blue polyester suit and white vest. It's too hot for that, Ted thought.

"Everybody, this is Sasha." Paul grinned broadly.

Sasha dropped to the floor.

"Did she hit her head?" Ted asked.

"Hell of an entrance," said a man at the table.

Ted's girlfriend, Mary, who had brought him to this place to meet her friends, came into the room. She was followed by Mike and Quinn, her buddies from school who leased the apartment.

"Get some ice," Mary said.

"No, she's all right," Paul said. Paul helped Sasha up. "Here, Sasha, take another one of these," he said.

"She don't seem to need another one of them," Mike said.

"Christ," Quinn said. "Bring her into the living room where it's cooler."

Sasha twisted and screamed. Her dark face contorted so that the left side seemed sectioned into tropical fruit–colored triangles.

"Where've you been?" Ted asked.

"To a funeral, man," Paul said over his shoulder.

He and Mary led Sasha into the living room. Mike and Quinn trailed after them. Ted asked the men at the table if they knew who had died.

"Must be that guy who killed himself," one said. "It was in the papers. Paul knew him."

"Was she related to him?"

"I don't know. Must've been something. Chick acting like that."

Paul was in the doorway loosening his tie. "Man, give me some of that," he said. He sipped Ted's drink. "It's this heat. She's real upset."

"Who died?" Ted asked.

"Her sister's boyfriend. That was an embarrassing funeral. A damn fight broke out, chicks and everything."

The men put their cards facedown on the table. Paul took off his coat, sat beside Ted on the low twill couch, and sipped again from Ted's drink.

"What happened?" Ted asked.

"It's a good thing it wasn't more crowded," Paul said. "The heat, you know, and a bunch of fancy-dressed women and some hustler types. The dead dude's mama and sister were up front, dressed all straight, sitting all by themselves. The preacher was going on about everlasting life. I'm hoping the corpse don't get up, you know?"

"What about the fight?"

"A trip. That started when the pallbearers were taking the casket out." Paul finished off the piña colada. Soft Latin jazz started up in the living room. "They'd gotten to the church door when Sasha's sister rushed one of the pallbearers.

"'Watch out, bitch,' the guy said. She had her nails in his neck, man. He dropped his part of the weight, and the casket lurched over. The other brothers were on their knees trying to hold it.

"'Murderer, murderer.' She screamed it. Real vicious. And the guy she attacked is shaking her by her wrists. Shakes her hat off."

"It wasn't suicide?"

"Officially. So now the dead guy's sister grabs Sasha's sister's hair, and they slap each other a few times. Everybody is yelling. The preacher, who has been bringing up the rear droning the 'heaven's wonderful' routine, gets between the two women.

"'Lord Christ,' he says. 'What is the matter with you?'

"The two sisters look at each other, breathing hard, looking stunned. The dead guy's sister says, 'I'd like to know what's wrong with this girl, here. My brother is in that casket, girl. This is my brother's funeral.'

"Both of them start crying. Sasha's sister turns to me, and then hugs Sasha and just boo-hoos. The other girl stands there staring at the casket. All six pallbearers are holding on with two hands now. They're sweating, and the one is bleeding onto his collar. They put the casket in the hearse, and Sasha faints. When I look around, Sasha's sister is riding off in a Lincoln with another woman and two men."

"Was the guy murdered or what?" Ted asked.

"Beats me, man. He was a criminal all right. All I know is that the guy was found dead with a bullet in his head."

Ted went into the kitchen and poured himself another drink from the pitcher of piña colada in the refrigerator. He peeped into the living room, where a floor fan and drawn shades cooled the space. Sasha was right in front of him, slumped on a dove gray sofa with maroon pillows. She was crying. Paul dried her cheeks with a pink hand-kerchief. Mike and Quinn sat behind the sofa on rattan stools. Mary beckoned Ted to sit by her on the floor. From the record player, a Brazilian male singer sang a love song in Portuguese.

Sasha took the handkerchief from Paul and wiped her nose. She sniffed. "I'm acting like my cousin," she said.

"Who?" Paul asked.

"The one that had a nervous breakdown. She got real fat. She got real fat and then she got real happy. I knew something was wrong."

"What was wrong?"

"Overactive gland. We used to go out together, but I stopped."

"I see."

"She scared me. The last time I saw her she was sitting on her porch. She looked stuffed with sand. I didn't know her at first. There was a full moon out. She had bright red lips and wore thick mascara. She said the moon looked like the back of a skull." Sasha shivered and frowned. "It did, too. White and small. She said she didn't trust anybody. She wasn't real happy anymore."

"But she was still real fat," Paul said.

"Yeah."

"You're not acting like that."

"But I'm not acting normal."

Ted got up and went into the den. He was asked if he wanted to play more cards, and he said no. He noticed that the plants in the room were remarkably healthy. On the wall, above a yucca, was a framed collage of fabric and photographs. He heard Sasha start to cry again. He tried to imagine being that emotional. He wondered if she was pretending, if she was nuts, if she was truly in pain.

He re-entered the living room to see Mary place a dampened cloth to Sasha's forehead. Paul sat with his arm around her shoulders.

"I don't belong anywhere," Sasha said. "Nobody cares."

"Nonsense," Paul said.

"No it's not," she said. "Nobody ever cared about me."
She pressed her face to a pillow and sobbed.

"She's right," Paul whispered to Mary.

Quinn offered to let her lie down in the bedroom, but
Sasha refused with a shake of her head.

"I'll take her home in a minute," Paul said.

Ted looked at her sparse, blue, open-toed shoes over-
turned on the worn Persian rug. She brought her shiny
bare legs from under her on the sofa and put her feet on
the floor. There was a thin gold ring around the middle
toe of each foot. She lifted her face from the pillow. The
silk flowers dangled from her loosened hair.

"Thank you," Sasha said. "I feel better now. I'm sorry
I'm such a mess. It's just everybody in my family is crazy.
I think my sister killed her boyfriend." She added quickly,
"I shouldn't have said that." She gazed at Ted with red
eyes. "People shouldn't have funerals," she said.

"Let me get you a cold drink," Ted said.

In the kitchen, he opened a cabinet of spices and then
found the glasses. He wondered whether to give Sasha
liquor. He stared into the refrigerator at the piña colada, a
gallon jug of apple cider, and a carton of milk. He decided
water would be best. He twisted ice from a tray, put some
cubes in a glass, and ran water from the tap. The door of
the freezer compartment swung out and bumped a hanging copper basket of peppers and onions.

When he gave Sasha the water, she had a picture book
of Morocco on her lap. Mary had crossed the room with
Mike to choose another album. Paul conferred with Quinn
behind the couch.

"I'd like to change," Sasha said.

"What you are wearing is lovely," Ted said.

"No. I'd like to change. You know, myself."

"Oh."

"I hate myself. I don't like any of you people, and you've all been so kind to me." She drank from the glass without looking up from the book.

"That's awful," Ted said.

"You don't like me either, do you?"

"I thought I might. I can wait if you want."

"Well, I'd like to change first. I've been told that I can." She smiled at Ted, and Ted smiled back. "This is hell," she said.

She traced the photograph of a veiled woman with her fingernail, putting in a nose and lips. Ted saw Mary peeping at them, and thought she could be jealous. Paul came over with Quinn and asked if she was ready to leave.

"Give me another pill," she said. He did, and she swallowed it with the water, then crunched a cube of ice. She held out her tongue with the ice crystals on it, and then washed them down with more water.

"You never dreamed you'd meet me," she said to Ted.

The card players came into the living room on their way out of the apartment. Each shook hands with Mike in a different way, and the one with the rubber fish hugged Quinn good-bye. He had the fish stuck under his belt at the side. When Mike closed the door behind them, Sasha said, "When I'm dead, I'll be dead. I want no one to carry my coffin."

"O.K.," Mary said, dropping the tone arm onto a record.

"I want belt fish to sing my eulogy."

"Let's go home," Paul said.

"No," Sasha said. She was laughing, and to Ted, she looked thoroughly tropical. "I want belt fish flung all around me."

Everyone laughed. The music of Betty Carter came from the speakers, high-pitched, bluesy and plaintive.

"Ziploc me," Sasha said.

Mary turned up the volume on the stereo and sat beside Sasha and the book about Morocco. They exchanged addresses. Mike, Quinn, and Paul began to dance, with Mike in front of Quinn, and Paul at her back. Ted sat on the floor and put his hand in one of Sasha's small shoes. Sasha puckered her lips at Mary, and Mary kissed her quickly on the mouth. Sasha showed Ted a page in the book with a rough, white stone wall and a heavy red door. "I want a door like that," Sasha said.

PRESENCE

I'm out near the pool holding a handful of ratchet sockets, watching Spike change the plugs and filters on the used LTD he has bought from a welder this morning, when Danny, this guy we don't know too well, comes sauntering out of his apartment carrying a six-pack of bottled beer. We've seen Danny in the pool back when it was warmer, and we know that he laughs a lot and drives an eighteen-wheeler. He usually parks it over by the fence and it takes up a lot of space, but it's not there today. I've bummed a smoke from him once or twice and he's bummed one from me.

He is already drinking one of the beers, and he offers one to Spike and me. He sets the six-pack on the pavement by the right front tire and sort of rotates his shoulders, like his back hurts. But he's smiling as always, his blond eyebrows kind of naturally arched with amusement.

"I'm going to Myrtle Beach at four in the morning," he says.

"Business or pleasure?" I ask.

"Work. Coming right back tomorrow night. But I hate to think there won't be some fun."

I touch Spike's arm with a cold bottle and he tells me to set it down until he's finished. So I put the ratchet sockets in my pocket and start drinking the beer myself.

"Where's your truck?" I ask Danny.

"I ain't driving," he says. "They took my license away some more yesterday. My damn sister. She's thirty-eight years old with two teenage boys and still living at home. My folks went to Oklahoma for a visit so I called the house for three hours yesterday to check on her, and the line was busy the whole time. So I put in an emergency call, and the operator said my sister was hanging up but she never did. It's because of her that I left home. We've gotten her jobs, I don't know how many, and she's quit or got fired from each one. I set her up with a buddy of mine who's a multimillionaire, got her moved in with him, and she even messed that up.

"So I went over there and she wouldn't open the doors. She could see it was me, and I could see her walking around checking the windows, all the while with the phone to her ear. I said, 'This is my daddy's house. This ain't your house. You can't lock me out.' Two days before that I went over there and she was remodeling the kitchen, soon as they had left. There she was painting the wallpaper, making the kitchen like she wanted it to be. I didn't want to call out to Oklahoma, 'cause my daddy's got a bad heart — he's had one heart attack already. Everybody knows my sister is trying to kill him. He's been supporting her and her boys forever and she won't do nothing to help. I went around to the bathroom — this was yesterday again — where the phone won't reach and climbed in the window. She yelled at me, asking what I thought I was doing, and I said I was taking out the phone.

"I went down to the basement where the main line is and she came up behind me and hit me on the head and neck with a metal pipe. I popped her on the forehead like this. Pop, you know, and that got her off me, knocking her back some. I didn't hit her hard like you hit a man, but she said she was gonna call the police. I'm thinking, This is my daddy's house. So I said, 'Call the police. That's right. Just call the police.'

"They pulled up out front in two cars and I went out there and invited them in. I wasn't scared, but you know what presence they have with all that heavy leather and metal and wood hanging on them. I don't know why she called them, and I told them that. 'This is just a family thing,' I said. 'I don't know why she called you. This ain't even her house.'

"'What is your name, sir?' one of them said.

"'My name is the same as my daddy's,' I said. 'This is my daddy's house.'

"'Do you mind stepping into another room while we talk to the lady?' he said.

"So I did. Then she told them I was drunk and didn't have a license. My license was revoked last year and I was doing all right with only a month to go. I know she told

them that, 'cause I read her lips through the French doors;
I know she did. Hell, I was standing there with a beer in
my hand, the same beer I climbed through the window
with and the same I had when I met the cops outside. I
wasn't no way drunk. The police motioned for me to come
back in and said to me, 'Do you have somewhere you can
go sleep tonight?' I mean they saw I was drinking. I wasn't
going nowhere, you know what I'm saying? They'd get
me for DWI as soon as I cranked up.

"I told them I didn't have no place to go. She told them
I did; I told them I didn't. So they left. I waited about
fifteen or twenty minutes while my sister was locked in
the bedroom and as soon as I got to the top of the hill there
they were, the same police. She's gonna pay for that. She
likes to dye her hair, so I'm gonna get some of that Neet
hair remover and put it in her hair dye. Or maybe I'll get
some peroxide and turn her hair as white as the witch's
hair ought to be, but that might get in her eyes and mess
her up, so I'll get some Neet. So long as she knows it's me
that did it.

"The one police who'd been doing all the talking took
me downtown and on the way I cried like a baby. I didn't
want to go to jail. That's why I'm standing here right now.
I'm standing here, right? By the time we got to the station
I had told that policeman my whole life's story 'cause I'm
trying to make him cry, too. But I'll fix her good. I hate to
think that I won't. Myrtle Beach is a long way and I'm
glad not to drive, you know? So I'll have my pleasure,
that's for sure."

Danny takes a swig of his beer and looks at me like it's

time for me to speak, but I don't know what to say. Spike is still under the hood, and I'm wondering about that sister, like what is her name and how to warn her about Danny. Then I decide to let it drop. I hold out my Newports and Danny takes one. The whole thing is none of my business.

Danny walks around the car sliding his hand over the surface, which is candy-apple red with flecks of gold. Spike pulls up from under the hood and gets himself a beer out of the carton.

"Thanks," he says to Danny.

"Start it," Danny says, nodding to the car. "Let's go get some more. Let's see how this beauty sounds. I got most of the day."

I AND I

You would like to go home. These drug runs are getting tiring. Besides, Mississippi makes you nervous. You look past your sun-darkened elbow out the window of the van at the house Rusty has sent you to. It is low, thick-looking, and made of red brick. Looks like a kiln. Stiff yuccas sprout from the bristling yard, and a dead palm tree bends against the right corner of the house. Timmy leans his sweaty face from the back, over your shoulder. "Rusty sure know how to pick 'em, don't he?" he says, breathing hotly on your ear.

Joyless puts the van in reverse and backs into the driveway, hiding the out-of-state license plates. His dreads hang heavy on his shoulders, and flop rigidly when he moves his head. You don't envy his heat. His hair is seasoned copper-colored, today like a network of heated wires. He brushes back the locks and steps from the van. For a moment, you

look out across the highway at the red neon beer sign in
the window of the convenience store. Timmy nudges you
and says, "Let's go."

Joyless has the key and opens the door. The house is
unfurnished, with many rooms. The front room is lavender with a wide brick fireplace, and the air is stuffy and
dim. While Timmy finds the thermostat and turns on the
air conditioning, you walk through the house as if inspect-
ing a hotel. You can't imagine anyone living here. Every
room is a different color — carpets purple, pink, blue,
green. Matching drapes shaped like suffocation hang in the
windows. They have funeral parlor folds, garish colors of
Dracula lips.

"I'll take the green room," Joyless says.

"The blue one for me," Timmy says.

You have your pick of the reds. You choose the front
room because it is near a door and has lavender blinds
instead of drapes.

When everyone awakens you are joined in the front
room, listening to your cassette player, your quart of beer
half empty. Your friends are barefoot and naked to the
waist. Their long toes sink deep into the carpet, leaving
dark, clawlike scars.

"I'm hungry," you say. "We passed a Morrison's on the
way."

"That should do," Joyless says, sitting down cross-legged
opposite you, his silver scimitar swinging from the thin
chain around his neck.

"I'm hungry to leave this place," Timmy says. "In my
sleep I heard screaming. How many brothers been offed in
this state?"

"Those were bats you heard," you say. "In the chimney, there."

The screeches sound from the chimney, and Timmy covers his ears. "No sleep for me tonight," he says. You look at Joyless and smile.

Joyless wears his name in Arabic on a Timmy-made silver bracelet. He reaches under his hair and pulls out a joint. He smokes hard until his head is lost in a cloud, a ragged orb of smoke. He passes the joint to Timmy. "I caught some lizards," he says. "Built a cage for them. There's all kinds of junk out back."

He gets up and returns with a makeshift wire mesh cage housing two small lizards and dried grass and sticks. He sets it down and the lizards turn bright green. "For the children," he says. "When we get home."

"They won't survive that long," Timmy says, twisting a short strand of his own early dreads. "Not through Florida and then all the way back."

"We'll feed them," Joyless says.

You wonder if Timmy's four-year-old would be afraid of them. You envision her stomping the cage determinedly the way she stomps on ants.

In Morrison's, Joyless has his hair under a brown knit hat so that his head looks like a beehive. He chooses french fries and vegetables, and nods at a couple pointing at him. He is used to it, and takes off the hat. Timmy chooses fish, and you take the chicken with a dish of cherry Jell-O filled with cottage cheese. You get two glasses of water and notice the check-out girl staring.

"Your hair," she says to Joyless. "What do you do with

it?" She is a pretty girl with yellowish skin and water-bright eyes.

Joyless gives her a steely look. "What do you think?" he says. "They are antennae tuned to black hole mystery. They drip honey. Lie down, I'll show you what I do with them."

"Very interesting. I guess you have to get used to it, huh?"

"It grows on you," Joyless says.

The girl gives him his price total, and Joyless finds a table by a wall. He is thin, and seems to spring when he walks, his long feet slewed in blue canvas shoes.

You give the girl your address and invite her over tonight. Timmy talks to her awhile about friends of hers.

At the table you wonder why no one else is staring. The room is nearly full. Old women with ice blue or blond hair, and men in farmer caps, hunch over their plates. Parents coax their children to eat. And teenagers wearing university T-shirts gesture brusquely with their forks. If you were them, you think, you would stare. You and your friends are not a complementary sight.

"Could be these folks are culturally deprived," Timmy says.

Joyless spreads his arms to take in the whole room. "I and I," he says.

"I think that girl might show tonight," you say.

You drink a full glass of water, take a breath, and start on the other one. Your tongue is cold. You lick your lips and catch the eye of the check-out girl.

"Much love and fear in her," Joyless says. "She won't come without a crowd."

"Let's hope not," Timmy says. "I need a party to help keep me awake."

"We have drugs for that," Joyless says. "And you have to drive tomorrow. Sleep."

"Not with bats in the tomb."

You finish eating and leave the cafeteria. Outside is golden and ninety-three degrees. A time and temperature sign gives you the numbers in computer digitals. You complain about the heat, the lack of wind. You feel as if a rubber glove were fitted to your face.

"It's not hot, really," Timmy says. He has rolled up the sleeves of his T-shirt, and his face and shoulders shine. Joyless's knit hat hangs out the back pocket of his army camouflage pants. He lifts his face, his eyes closed, to the setting sun, and walks basking that way until you reach the van. Because of the heat, you dread getting into the van. It is a dark green Dodge with black carpet on the floor and interior walls. You offer to drive to avoid having to ride in the back, and Timmy grabs the passenger seat and turns on the radio, searching for "the black spot," he says. Joyless sprawls on the floor in the back between the two benchlike couches and lights up a joint. Before you leave the parking lot, he passes it to you. You would like to see a movie, to watch TV. "I wonder who won the Braves game," Timmy says.

When you get to the house, you walk across the highway to the convenience store to buy more beer. You think you should feel free, but you are vaguely frightened. Maybe you are developing agoraphobia. Heat waves rise from the pavement. A few cars whiz under the traffic light. Tall dry grass grows in the median. Small shirtless children play in the dirt yards of the project housing next to the store. You're glad you will never have to get used to this place.

The store is a Jr. Food Mart, with Jr. himself painted as a big, dark-haired Howdy Doody look-alike on the sign above the entrance. Inside, two musky little girls stand on bare tiptoes at the counter to buy lime-flavored Push-Ups and an assortment of grape and lemon candy. There is a different man at the cash register from when you were here before.

You get the beer from the glass-encased cooler. Just as you pull out a six-pack, another takes its place. Startled, you stand there until someone's hands appear behind the cans placing beer in the cooler from the back. "You scared me," you say, but the person doesn't answer. You take out another six-pack and go to the front.

At the counter, the little girls have left, and the attendant you thought was a man turns out to be a coal black young woman with a fresh, short haircut, and wearing a man's white tank-top undershirt. As she bags the beer you gaze at the dark nipples under the tight-fitting shirt.

"You're not from around here, are you?" she asks.

You try, but you can't think of anything. "I give up."

"Fifty-dollar bills are rare in this store. You here to stay or just passing through?"

"Spending the night."

"You're lucky." Two of her top front teeth are edged with gold. Her skin looks smooth and very soft.

"My friends and I are staying across the street. You should come over when you get finished here."

"Yeah? I was thinking about it. I saw you pull up over

there. We like to welcome new folks to the area, you know?"

You smile, take your change, and walk with the beer to the house. Joyless and Timmy are preparing the package of cocaine to be delivered. You tell them about the girl at the store, and Timmy is pleased, but Joyless looks annoyed.

You look at the Kleenex box he is wrapping with a sheet of newspaper.

"Timmy and I will make the delivery. You ought to hang around. Too many people know we're here already."

Joyless and Timmy are gone a long time. You look out back for crickets, and manage to catch another lizard, too. You put them all in the cage, and drink while listening to the tape player. It is a muffled tape recorded from the radio on a cheap cassette. When darkness falls, you look for lamps, but nothing is in the closets except empty coat hangers. You find a light bulb in the ceiling fixture of the green room, and you have to jump several times before unscrewing it. You use the same technique to install it in the front room ceiling. The bats start screeching, and you turn up the volume of the tape player.

Joyless and Timmy have been gone at least three hours. You wonder what you will do if it turns out they're busted. You try the radio to hear the time. You can't call the police. You will wait awhile longer and then call Rusty.

Car lights glance off the blinds, and you turn down the music to listen for the sound of the engine. It is not the van. A car door closes, and footsteps crunch on the gravel driveway. You go to the window and peep through a slit in the blinds. The car is a new Chevrolet, but you cannot see who is at the door. There is a knock and you leave the window. You wait for another knock but it doesn't come. Instead, there are footsteps again, and the close of the car door. You are afraid to go back to the window, not wanting to be seen. For a while the car sits in the driveway, the motor running. Then it leaves. The bats are screaming in the chimney.

You go through the house making sure all the doors and windows are locked, and you hide all the coke in your suitcase in a back closet. Then you turn off the light and peep out the window again, noticing that the convenience store is still open. Maybe the Chevy belonged to the girl at Morrison's. In the darkness, something tickles your foot, and you think maybe the lizards are loose. Hopping up, you turn on the light and see two roaches run to the corner of the room. You throw your shoe at them. The light stays on.

Your respect for Rusty is waning. You used to marvel at his resourcefulness, the way he always found you places to stay in any city you needed to visit. A Realtor friend who owed him a favor offered him this house with air conditioning or one with furniture. Right now you would like a rocking chair, and some pictures on the walls.

You lie with your ear to the tape player, eventually losing yourself in the reggae. You must have dozed, because someone is at the door again. This time the van is out there. Timmy is calling your name.

You let them in. They stand on the threshold carrying brown sacks of cooking equipment and a two-pound bag of shrimp. Behind them the light of the convenience store is out. A car, the Chevy, pulls into the driveway behind the van. You all look, and the girl from Morrison's gets out. She is alone, and no longer in her green and white uniform; instead she is wearing blue shorts and a white jersey with the word *Bruisers* printed on the front.

"I'm a star," she says, shaking her fists above her head. "A grand slam in the bottom of the twelfth. How do you like me, guys?"

"I love a winner," Timmy says.

Joyless laughs and shakes her hand.

"Where've you guys been?" she asks. You ask if she likes shrimp.

Inside you boil the shrimp while the girl explains the tricks of playing third base for the B&G Grill Bruisers. *B&G* is printed in blue script on the back of the jersey above the number 12. Making sure she doesn't hear, you tell Joyless where the coke is, and he squats in the living room laying out lines on a mirror between his feet.

Soon, you and the girl serve up the shrimp, passing out paper plates and paper towels. Joyless sets aside the mirror of coke, and Timmy gets up to wash his hands. When he returns, the convenience store girl arrives, wearing a fresh tank top and loose white pants with orange birds printed on them. Timmy is delighted. He says he won't have to sleep with bats.

"Do you expect to sleep with me instead?" says the convenience store girl.

"Forgive me, no," Timmy says. "I won't have to sleep at all."

Soon there is a pile of shrimp skins on all the plates. Joyless talks about sleeping with the moon. "At night on the mountain you scoot over to make room for it, it rises so close. Then when morning, you look down through mist at lush green pasteled by a rainbow in the valley."

The softball girl wants to know what mountain.

"My mountain," Joyless says. "In Columbia."

"Joyless is from Boston," you say. "He has multiple biographies."

"I'm a talented surgeon," he says.

"We are house painters on vacation," Timmy says. "On our way to Florida. You ladies care to come along?"

They both say they can't.

You go over and thump the lizard cage. They are either dead or asleep, turned dark gray. You remember the bright green of their day. You thump some more. The convenience store girl moves over and kneels beside you. Suddenly one of the lizards brightens, and its throat swells flashing red. "It has a song inside," she says. You look at her as if she is crazy.

You stay up late doing the coke. The girls talk about their town. They had never met before, having gone to different high schools, but they have seen each other at parties. They say how much they want to travel, and you and Timmy make them like you with tales of big cities. Joyless is a mystic and a poet, you say. And a terrible painter. When he paints walls he paints the windowpanes, too, and you have to clean it off. They laugh and like Joyless, too. Timmy gets out his kit and shines his silver jewelry. He gives each girl a ring he has made.

They leave before sunup, and you search for another cassette to play, something you haven't heard. Joyless puffs on a large joint, the smoke curling in his hair like a ghost wig. Everything is always strange, you think. The bats, for now, are quiet.

Timmy bends to the mirror on the carpet and pulls up his eyelid. He turns his head from side to side and then lifts the other lid. "Home they hiring at Lockheed," he says.

Joyless takes another big puff. You stare at Timmy, wondering if he would really go to work. Joyless passes you the joint. He smiles at you and looks at the cage. "Let's paint it," he says.

ON EARTH

One night in January, when Sam was nineteen, he was awakened from the den sofa by his parents, who were escorting each other to the kitchen for a midnight dose of Maalox. They stood over him in their baggy pajamas, their faces lined and puffy from sleep, his father telling him to get into bed. Without their partial dentures, eyes heavy-lidded, in the monochrome light of the signed-off TV, they were old for the first time. Sam was so startled that he laughed.

By February, he was ninety miles from home, in another town. Then, late that summer, he started night school and his efficiency apartment went condo. Going to night school meant he had to learn to study, if he really wanted a promotion to full machinist, which he did, and the condo conversion meant he had to find a cheaper place to live. The promotion would be his ticket out of the rock quarry.

He worked there as a machinist's assistant, which meant that he fetched tools, cleaned up the work area, and got out of the way when giant earthmovers — guided by wild and idiotic drivers needing a blade repaired — rumbled into the shop at daredevil speeds.

The quarry itself was harmful to his sensibility, as he put it — colorless, noisy, and hard. It was the landscape of death, and he linked it with his parents, whose deaths he had left home to escape. But once he was a qualified machinist he could work anywhere, somewhere closer to life.

By contrast, night school was paradise. There was indeed color — orange and blue vinyl furniture, and polished yellow hallways under bright fluorescent lights. And there were friendly young black women, in vivid summer clothes and sandals — women miles away from the wan, lank-haired machinists' wives who sometimes drove to the quarry to drop off lunch and joke with everybody but him. It was a place where he could wear regular sports shirts or, for his machinist's class, orange denim overalls, rather than the gray uniform of the quarry.

It was by following a woman that he found his new dwelling. He had taken off from the quarry to register for classes, and had zoned in on a girl in a silver spandex suit. He stood behind her in a course-card line, and acted nonchalant about the smooth, shimmering curves of her hips. He overheard what course she asked for, and when his turn came he asked for the same. While standing in line for his machine-shop course, he kept an eye on her, waiting until she was finished with her enrollment, so that he could follow her out of the gym. She tacked a note to the bulletin board in the hall, and after she left the building he snatched the note down. She had a room to rent.

Half an hour later, he called her number from a pay phone in the canteen. A woman answered, but she sounded old — too weary for a girl. He explained that he was a student, got the address, and walked right over. The house was across the street from the campus.

The woman he had spoken to came to the door. She was broad-shouldered and had waxy, light skin. She looked to Sam like a thick cinnamon candle dressed in a rose-print housecoat.

"Something smells good," Sam said on her threshold.

"It doesn't happen all the time," Mrs. Finn said.

"I don't want any. A cake, right? It just sure smells good is all I'm saying."

"It's for my grandson, Hugh. His school's fund-raiser."

"He lives here?"

"And his mother, my daughter."

"His mother, your daughter?"

"Tina."

The house was spotless, and newly decorated with sea green carpeting and hint-of-peach paint. A plastic runner stretched down a hall from the front door to the kitchen.

"I like things tidy," Mrs. Finn said. "You're the only roomer I've had. At first I wanted a girl — someone who could look after Hugh once in a while. But girls can be a big responsibility if they're all by themselves. Of course, I didn't know what kind of person might call. I've got the right to refuse, though."

"I like kids pretty much," Sam said.

"Well, I got some rules just the same."

Sam stood behind a plump, rosy sofa in the living room. Most of the furniture was big and antique — a green armchair, framed in dark wood like the sofa, and cherry tables with curved legs.

"Are you listening?" She said he couldn't use the front door or the kitchen door. And he couldn't use the kitchen — she and Tina shouldn't have to be dressed just to get coffee in the morning or a snack at night. He'd have to limit his guests; she was used to a quiet house. He couldn't use the phone, so he would have to get his own installed. He certainly shouldn't answer her phone under any circumstances when he was home alone, since it might be a long-distance call for a regular household member.

"Could I bring food into my room?"

She trailed her fingers down the front of her neck. "Don't leave any for ants."

Mrs. Finn started down the hall, and Sam followed her. Pausing at the stairs, she pointed out Tina's and Hugh's rooms — beside one another at the bottom of the steps.

"Tina's at work by now. Selling Pontiacs. She's taking classes at Tech herself. Hugh's at school. Kindergarten." She hesitated, her hand on the banister, and turned her gaze on Sam. "I have respect for people who want to learn. Better themselves. Tina's doing it. I always wanted to myself."

She led him up to see his room. It was refurbished attic space, with a sloping ceiling, shiny wood floors, and white walls. There was an old, newly varnished bed with carved pineapples in its headboard. As Mrs. Finn pulled back the curtain from a glass-paneled door, Sam saw metal fire escape steps and the black shingled roof of the neighbor's house.

"I think you'd be comfortable here," Mrs. Finn said. "There's a closet and a bathroom. You might need a basket for your dirty clothes. There's a laundry room on the campus, I believe."

Sam asked how much she was charging, and she told him.

"That's a little high," he said. "Maybe I could do some chores to trim that price. I have a car."

"I don't want you to think I need a man around here. The last happiest day of my life was when Mr. Finn left. I don't cherish any memories of a man around the house. Tina's husband was no better than mine. If you see any one of them coming, you stay away. That's what I tell Hugh, and that's what I tell you."

"Do they live near here?"

"They live together, of all things. Across town. I wonder how they live at all."

She sat down on the foot of the bed and smoothed her housecoat over her knees. "Do you have parents?" she asked.

"Not here. I've been on my own for six months. My daddy told me to shape up or ship out. But he said it in a nice way. He was daring me, you know. So I decided to ship out and shape up."

Mrs. Finn stared at him. "Are you a good boy?" she asked.

"Sure. Pretty good. I work down at the quarry. I'm learning a trade. I've got ambitions. I'd say I'm pretty good. Even my daddy would say that."

"Well, I could let you use the phone to call your folks — collect, I mean. To let them know where you are, assuming you want the room."

"I want it, all right. The money is right here." He patted his back pocket. "But I can wait till I get my own phone."

The next time Sam saw Tina was the following night, in class. It was an early childhood development class. He was one of two men there, not counting the teacher, who was portly and knock-kneed and called everybody Dollface. Tina sat in the front row, in a slim aqua dress and low-heeled shoes. When the teacher asked her why she was taking the course, she put her hands to her cheeks and squeezed her face.

"That's an easy one, Dollface," the teacher said.

Tina kept squeezing. All Sam could see of her face was her right ear, which had three gold loops along the curve.

"I'll ask someone else," the teacher said. "You get a grip on yourself."

Most people said they wanted to teach, and Sam just said that he was curious. He spent his time thinking of what he would say to Tina after class, and staring at the back of the head of the man in front of him. A pair of dice was neatly etched in his hair, showing snake eyes.

The teacher got back to Tina. She squeezed her face again, but stopped suddenly and spoke up. She said she wanted an associate degree in nursing, and that she had a five-year-old son, and that the course would be a big help to her. The teacher dropped his jaw and bugged out his eyes. "Incredible," he said, and began an overview of the course.

During a break in the class, Sam had his chance to speak to Tina. She was in the hall, bumming a cigarette from the guy with the haircut. He introduced himself, and asked if she was all right.

"She's fine," the guy said. "A little shy, maybe. My name is Bullet. This is Tina."

"I know. I live at her house."

"You *do?*" Tina said.

"Yep. Small world, isn't it?"

"Claustrophobic," Bullet said.

"So you're the rock worker," Tina said.

"Actually, I work with metal. Cutting and welding. At the quarry."

"So why are you in this class?"

"Like I said. I have an interest. I'm complex like that."

"Not your average bear," Bullet said to Tina.

"And you're not your average hair," Tina said.

Bullet ran his hand over his head and grinned. "I try," he said.

"So Tina," Sam said. "When this is all over, maybe I could walk you home."

"If it's not out of your way," Bullet said.

"I can be kind," Sam said.

The teacher came out of the room and pointed to them. "O.K., Dollfaces. It's showtime," he said.

■

The street between the campus and the house was a wide, four-lane drag. Sam and Tina stood at the curb waiting for the traffic to die. A mile or so away — beyond a block of houses and the campus buildings — the lighted orange and yellow signs of fast-food restaurants fed into the horizon.

"Are you hungry?" Sam asked.

"No. But you'd better get something now, since you can't use the kitchen."

"I already ate. Your mother's pretty strict. Which makes me wonder how you have a kid at your age, and how you get to look so sexy all the time."

"I'm older than I look. Too old for you, in case you're wondering that, too."

"Yeah, I'm wondering that." He hopped up and down twice, turning his head both ways to look at the whizzing cars. "Traffic always like this? Let's go."

He grabbed her hand and they ran across the highway, leapt the curb, and stopped at the brick porch steps.

Sam looked up at the front door, its warm porch light. "Come up to my room," he said.

Tina sat down on the step and squeezed her face. She had an asymmetrical hair style — short on one side and long on the other, like a sideswiped mushroom. When she spoke, her voice was muffled by her hands. "Look. You don't have to live here. You can get lost."

"Is that what you told your husband? What do you tell Bullet?"

"Bullet *is* my husband." She kept her hands to her face.

He started around the side of the house to the fire escape

steps but came back. "You don't want to do that," he said, pulling one of her hands down. "How do you sell cars and do that?"

"Mama talks too much." The hand went back to her face. "I don't sell cars. I'm a hostess there, very part-time. I get coffee for customers."

"Still. It's a shame."

"I want to be tiny. I'm making myself tiny."

"You *are* tiny."

"Well, I want to disappear, then. Actually, I want my own galaxy."

Sam laughed and sat down beside her. "I apologize," he said. "You're pretty is all I've been saying." He reached to flick dirt off his tennis shoe. Tina rested her chin on her fist.

"Mama's crazy to rent the room to you."

"I told her I like kids. It's true."

She studied his face. He wanted her to believe him, and he didn't know whether or not to smile. He did.

"What do you want, Sam? This kid's-world class you're taking with me won't help you cut metal. You're not as complex as you are jive."

He gazed off toward the street and followed the red taillights of a car until he lost them among a glimmering pool of others. "World peace," he said, and slapped his thigh.

Tina groaned and rolled her eyes.

"No? All right. I want to be like my dad. No joke. He's confident. He's cozy. He's got his own galaxy."

"Maybe I should meet him. What does he do?"

"He's a supermarket butcher. You should see what he eats for breakfast."

She squeezed her face again.

"I think I want to be like Bullet," he said. "He's got you in his orbit."

"He sells watches and gold chains at barbershops. Has a three-county territory. The husband part doesn't mean much. He shows up for birthdays. Said today he wants to get to know me better."

"You going to let him?"

"He knows me already. You never will, and I have a class in the morning."

She stood and stepped up to the porch. Sam turned sideways and watched her. "At least I have a place to live," he said. "I'm going to dream about you."

"You'd better study," she said, and went inside the house.

For two weeks, Sam studied. He learned something about what children do when, and the safety precautions for welding. Then, one day, Mrs. Finn was dead. For how long no one was sure. Paramedics revived her, but she was still unconscious when Sam learned about her stroke. Brain damage would be a concern if she survived. Bullet phoned him at the quarry, described the police cars in the driveway and the ambulance in the yard, neighbors and students milling around the front of the house, Tina's astonishing control. She had found her mother in convulsions when she came home from her morning class. By the time she called the ambulance and her father, her mother lay still.

Dead. And she stayed that way until the rescue squad succeeded in bringing her around. Bullet wanted to know if Sam could get off early to look after Hugh when he got home from school.

The day at the quarry had seemed interminable, as usual. Sam had painted the two trash barrels that flanked the shop's vehicle entrance safety Day-Glo green, stretching the chore to take up three hours. Then he tried to hide the fact that he had nothing to do. After Bullet called, he spoke to the shop foreman, punched out, and left the gray expanse of the quarry, feeling both relief and dread as the sky turned bluer along the tree-lined street to town.

He found the storm door propped open. Tire tracks matted the grass in the yard. The front door was unlocked. Torn glassine wrappers littered the hallway runner, and Tina's schoolbooks lay thrown against the living room sofa. Mrs. Finn's bedcovers were twisted. He made the bed, picked up the wrappers, and stacked Tina's books. Then he fixed an apple-jelly sandwich for Hugh.

As he cleaned jelly droplets off the kitchen counter, Hugh's bus pulled up. Sam watched from the living room window as the boy waved at the bus and ran to the porch. He carried a Ninja book bag and wore high-top tennis shoes printed with multicolored dinosaurs.

"I've been wondering about you," Hugh said as Sam opened the door for him. He threw his book bag over the back of the sofa. His hair was cut clean on the sides, but it was curly on top, and he had a short, braided rattail at the nape of his neck.

"Me, too," Sam said. "About you."

"Where's Grandma?"

"She got sick. She's at the hospital. She'll be back."

"When?"

"I don't know. Your mom, dad, and grandpa are with her. You want a sandwich?"

"Can I watch cartoons?"

"What would your grandma say?"

Hugh looked into Mrs. Finn's bedroom. He shrugged, tilting his head to one shoulder and smiling crookedly. He had perfect little teeth and eyelashes like a girl's.

"I don't care," Sam said.

There was a five-inch color TV on the kitchen counter, and Hugh ran to turn on a show called "TigerSharks." He poured milk into a Barney Rubble glass and took his sandwich to a Big Bird placemat at the kitchen table.

"You learn anything at school?" Sam asked.

"We went to India on magic carpets."

Hugh kept his eyes on the TV screen, which featured manfish monsters plotting the theft of a cloaking device. He ate from the center of his sandwich, to avoid the thick-crusted edges. "We saw animals and we talked about them," he said.

"I'll bet that was fun."

"I almost fell off the carpet."

Sam put the jelly jar back into the refrigerator and took out a package of sliced turkey for himself.

"The circus is coming," Hugh said. A commercial showed a flipping aerial act. "I can do that. I want to go there."

The phone in the hallway rang. It was a neighbor asking

about Mrs. Finn. Sam wrote down her name, and as soon
as he hung up the phone rang again. It was Tina this time.
She asked about Hugh, and said her mother was still in a
coma. Sam tried to imagine Tina squeezing her face with
a phone to her ear.

"We're O.K. here," Sam said. "Your mother needs you
there tonight."

"I'm coming on home. I have to get Hugh ready for
school tomorrow."

From the hallway, Sam saw Hugh standing on a stool,
looking at a calendar over the kitchen sink.

"Take your time," he said to Tina, and hung up. He
went back into the kitchen and ate a slice of turkey. Hugh
leaned over the sink, resting one hand on the windowsill
and lifting the pages of the calendar with the other.

"Get down from there," Sam said.

Hugh turned around and crouched as if ready to jump.
"Watch this," he said.

Sam pushed quickly from the counter and caught Hugh
in midflip.

Hugh was settled in front of the big color TV in Mrs.
Finn's bedroom when Tina got home. She brought Bullet
and her father, a short, burly man wearing a brown three-
piece corduroy suit. Sam gave Tina the neighbor's message
and went up to his room. He lay on his bed and tried to
memorize the parts of a lathe pictured in his textbook —
lines were drawn from sections of the machine to numbers
scattered all about the page. In a while, he fell asleep and
dreamed that he was sitting on the top landing of the fire

escape watching a giant passenger plane fly low over the campus buildings, heading his way. He saw clearly into the cockpit, where his father and mother were smiling and waving at him. The plane dipped sideways, so that he could see its dazzling silver underbelly, and crashed on the other side of the house next door. Gray quarry dust rose up from the wreckage, then sifted down on him. The plane's huge wing protruded over the black roof of the neighbor's house, blocking out everything else behind it, and sirens sounded in the distance.

The odd, disturbing calm he felt in the dream stayed with him when he awoke. There were no actual sirens. The house was quiet. He turned on the light by his bed and rushed to take a shower. He still had time to make shop class, and he left by the fire escape, with twilight in the sky, and heavy traffic busy on the street.

At the door of the shop building, he changed his mind about entering. He went to the canteen and called his parents from a pay phone. He told his father about his move, school, and Mrs. Finn. His father asked if he was all right.

"Sort of thrown for a loop is all."

"On the trail of an F-minus already?"

"I can handle this, O.K.?"

Sam heard a match strike. His father was lighting his pipe. "Are you on or off track?"

"What?"

"Do you know what you're doing?"

"I just told you what I'm doing. I'm going to hang up in a minute."

Sam heard his father's teeth click on the stem of the

pipe. The canteen was determinedly bright, with large rainbows painted on the walls.

"You ought to study refrigeration," his father said. "Better future."

"Yeah. Impressive, too."

"What happened to your landlady could happen to your mother or me," his father said.

"Don't you think I know that? I know that."

"How do I know what you know? You might have to move out of there. You know?"

"The kid will need taking care of until his grandma gets well."

There was a wheezing sound. His father either sighed or pulled on the pipe. "Do you cook?" his father asked. "What are you eating? Let me send you a package."

The operator told Sam to deposit more coins. Sam told his father good-bye.

He walked out under the globe lamps of the campus and remembered that he hadn't asked about his mother. He decided that it was much too late to go to class, so he would get his car and drive around. But when he crossed the street he saw Tina and the men in her life crowded on the small front porch. Bullet and Mr. Finn cradled brown paper bags. Tina wore a lemon yellow sweater. Hugh held the ear of a stuffed animal to his lips and leaned against his mother's leg while she peered into her purse.

Sam stood at the curb unnoticed by them, wondering if he could slip around to the fire escape without a greeting. Then Tina looked out, leaned forward with a squint, and called his name.

The porch was really too small for the five of them. Sam

stepped up, back down, and up again, trying to find a place to stand. Mr. Finn grabbed his wrist and maneuvered him flat against the storm door. "Do you gamble, Sam?" he asked. Bullet chuckled.

"Move, Sam," Tina said. She was smiling.

Sam lodged his shoulder between Bullet and Mr. Finn while Tina unlocked the door. The paper bag smelled of fried fish, and the men smelled of beer. They went inside and laid out fish dinners in white plastic boxes on the kitchen table.

"Dig in," Mr. Finn said. Under his suit he wore a pink shirt with an oversized collar and a wide paisley tie. "Eat up, Hugh."

Hugh grabbed a handful of french fries and spread them on his placemat. Bullet and Mr. Finn sat down, and Bullet made a sandwich of fish and white bread. Tina took her food to the counter, and Sam sat down across from Mr. Finn.

"Your mama's going to be fine," Mr. Finn said. "Did you hear what she said tonight? She said Ruth is still no good. Ruth's been dead ten years."

"Mrs. Finn is conscious?" Sam asked.

"Not really," Tina said. "She's out of the coma, but she was talking out of her head."

Sam watched Bullet take a gentle, expert bite of his sandwich, leaving a deep curve of cleanly exposed fish skeleton.

"But she's going to, you know, live," Sam said.

"She's already been dead," Mr. Finn said, forking up a mound of slaw. "She's got no choice."

Hugh handed Sam a packet of ketchup to open. The boy's cheeks were crammed with french fries, and he did his talking with his eyes, big and bright and innocently asking.

"She was talking crazy, though, Pop. We've got to think about brain damage," said Tina.

"She was talking about Ruth, for God's sake. The woman's observant. Always has been. She never did like your aunt, Tina, and you know it. Ain't nothing wrong with your mama's brain."

Sam got up to get a drink. He looked for a glass in the cabinet next to Tina, and with the open door concealing his face from the others he whispered, "Ruth's dead?"

She nodded solemnly.

"Let me squeeze your face," he said.

She punched him in the ribs. He filled his glass with tap water and sat back down. Bullet stared at him, his shoulders hunched, his hands deftly gripping the sandwich, in the midst of another delicate bite. Sam thought he could detect an old ace of diamonds on the top of his head.

Sam looked at Mr. Finn. "Why'd you ask if I gamble?"

"'Cause I used to. Used to go all over just gambling. You should move in with us, Sam. I've got trophies and plaques everywhere. It's really a beautiful place. Besides, you look like the daring type."

"Good idea," Bullet said.

"I don't think so," Sam said. "I like it right here right now. Though I'd like to see those trophies."

"Leave him alone, Pop," Tina said.

"Oh. Is he fragile or something?" Mr. Finn said.

"You're the flying man on the daring trapeze," Hugh said to Sam.

"Hugh wants to go to the circus," Sam said.

"What say we go swimming?" Mr. Finn said.

"Surfing's better," Bullet said.

"Skin diving," Mr. Finn said.

"Yachting," Bullet said.

"Just stop it," Tina said, her fists against her ears.

"Hang gliding," Hugh said.

Bullet took a handful of watches from his pocket. He held one up that had a silver-and-gold bracelet. "How much will you give me for this one?" he asked Sam.

"Nothing," Tina said. Her eyes were closed, and she rubbed her forehead with her wrist. "Hugh, Sam and I will take you to the park tomorrow."

"We will?" Sam asked.

Bullet dropped the watches on the table. "Do you think that's appropriate?" he asked.

"What's fun about the park?" Mr. Finn said.

"A Plexiglas tube you can slide through," Tina said. "It's twenty feet high."

"O.K., if you want. We'll all go," Mr. Finn said. "And we'll eat sugar all day."

"Really?" Hugh asked. He seemed bewildered, turning from one person to the next as if he didn't know what to trust.

"Maybe," Tina said.

"Absolutely," Sam said to Hugh. "Then we'll go see your grandma and tell her almost everything. We'll have the greatest time on earth."

SCUFF

Sarah lay on her bed studying a labor case when her brother, Mike, walked in.

"Sis," he said, picking at a scab on his elbow, "I have a learning disability."

"How do you know?" she asked, setting her glasses on top of her head.

"I heard it on television just now."

She got up, laughing, and hugged him. He was a big, unemployed nineteen-year-old who had been sent by their parents to live with her. It was hard to believe he got into so much trouble at home, because now he rarely left the apartment.

"Come on, Sis, let's wrestle." He spun her around and locked her arm behind her back. "This is Tyke Daniels making Masked Mountain eat dirt," he said, and crashed her onto the bed.

"Say, 'Love is a fresh bowl of slugs,'" he said. She tussled with him until the heavy books hit the floor and the thin pink bedspread was mussed.

"Love is a fresh bowl of slugs," she said, her head sore and caught in a leg lock.

"Say, 'I'll buy my gentle brother some wine,'" he said, tightening the vise about her ears.

"I'll buy my gentle brother some wine," she yelled.

He let her up and strutted around the bed, beating his chest. He scowled in front of an imaginary camera and challenged Ape-man Kanochi to a death match, ripping the buttons off his shirt and charging fiercely into the living room.

Sarah slammed the door and locked it.

When the phone rang, she hoped it was Duncan, her boss at the National Labor Board, where she was a rookie learning the rules of arbitration. She couldn't remember laughing, even at Mike, before she got close to Duncan. The worst part was that she had known he was married from the start. She didn't mind that he was twenty years older than she.

She answered the phone, and Duncan said, "You always sound surprised when you say hello."

"Mike says I sound sexy," she said.

"I want to see you. Meet me in my overcoat at quarter to nine."

She paused before answering. "O.K.," she said slowly. "I can tell Mike I'm going to buy wine."

She met him in the parking lot of the liquor store, and they drove to an alley and parked. It was the first time she confessed that she loved him.

That weekend, she and Mike cleaned up the apartment. He was really not an unpleasant boy, she thought. The two weeks he had been there he did everything she asked. He was anxious about Monday's stag lodge elections back home because he was on the ballot for secretary. Its members were a group of conservative old men who did nothing but get drunk every night. She couldn't understand why Mike wanted to be with them so much. She didn't think he was actually a member. He worked there as a bartender before he left home, and for some reason those old men liked him, which was partly why her parents had gotten him out of town.

While she was cleaning, she kept finding things broken, and Mike couldn't explain how they had gotten that way. She found a cracked vase on the bookshelf and a rip in the carpet by the television. She was dusting the frame holding a picture of their parents when the whole thing fell apart.

"My God, Mike. Do you play football in here when I'm gone? You're so damn lazy and clumsy."

"I'm sorry, Sis," he said, cleaning the television screen. "I didn't do it on purpose."

She remembered how he had broken her hairbrush and her favorite water pitcher, and she grew quietly angry. She jerked around the vacuum cleaner and switched it on. Everywhere she pushed it he seemed to be standing in the way. Once, she jammed it over his feet, and screamed, "Get out of here. Go home to your precious drunks."

He went into the kitchen. Sarah turned off the vacuum. She heard him pouring Froot Loops into a bowl. She went to him and thumped him lightly on the head. He took the cereal to the living room and watched tag team wrestling on the SuperStation.

Sarah traveled out of town on Monday to oversee a union vote. She drove the three hours back to the apartment hoping to get right into bed. Mike was sitting on the floor wearing headphones, with two empty wine bottles beside him, and a half-gallon bottle between his legs. The sofa was pulled crookedly into the middle of the room, and black scuff marks were on the wall.

"Mike, get your low-life butt off that floor," she said, pulling the earphones off his head.

"Aw, you sound just like Mama." His head lolled to the side.

"Why can't you act right? Look at that wall, Mike."

"I lost, Sis."

His drunkenness infuriated her. She kicked a wine bottle, and it smashed against the bookcase before she realized what he had said. He looked up at her as if he was going to cry.

"Was it close?"

"As close as Hitler and Santa Claus."

She sat beside him, stroked his hair, and took a swig from the bottle of Labrusca.

When she came home from work the next day, the scuff marks were gone and the broken glass was cleaned away. Mike was in the kitchen feeding milk to a strange gray cat.

"That guy just called," he said.

"What guy?" She knew it was probably Duncan because he never left his name, though Mike was certainly no threat. Duncan hadn't been at work that day, and she was worried that he was ill. Several times she almost called him, to report on her trip, she would say. But she could never convince herself that that was strong enough reason, and she hoped he would call her, instead.

He finally phoned again when she was drinking beer with Mike in the kitchen. Mike had the cat on the table, checking its ears for fleas. She couldn't stand the cat being on the table, but she didn't have the heart to say anything. The cat was dirty — a plain alley cat with dried, white wounds on its haunch. It was skinny and collarless, and she truly wished Mike wouldn't want to keep it.

Duncan wanted to take Sarah out to dinner, but she was dieting and didn't want to eat. The reason he wasn't at work was that his wife had broken her leg in a fall down their back porch steps. He had driven her to her sister's house, thirty-five miles away, so someone could care for her during the day.

"You're a very bad man," Sarah said.

"I know it," he said. "Why don't you come over here?"

"I'd have to think of something," she said, glancing at Mike, who was looking under the cat's tail.

"Say it's business. Say the president's been fired and you have to go handle the grievance."

"Can I call you back?"

"If you promise to bring me dinner."

She considered telling Mike that a girlfriend needed her, but he knew she didn't have close friends in town. She couldn't think of anything that would keep her out of the house for more than twenty or thirty minutes. It would be better, she thought, to see Duncan tomorrow — to go straight to his house from work.

She called him and told him.

"I'll come over there, then. I'll bring some folders to make it look good."

"That's an idea. Don't wear too much cologne."

"I'll step in dog shit if you want me to."

Duncan arrived wearing a green knit shirt, blue jeans, and Sperry Topsiders. This was the first time she had seen him dressed like that, and she thought he looked cute with his stomach bulging slightly under the shirt. She introduced him to Mike, who seemed unusually quiet.

"Where can we work?" Duncan asked.

She led him to the kitchen, while Mike turned on the TV and lay back petting the cat.

Duncan opened his briefcase on the table and kissed Sarah on the lips.

"Sis," he said. "May I call you Sis? You're great and gorgeous." He held her as she leaned against the counter under the Peanuts calendar.

"How's Barbara?" she asked.

"Ashamed," he said. "And loving all the attention." He wore rectangular, silver-rimmed glasses that made him look like a dentist to Sarah. She brushed the bright gray hair at his temples and kissed his stubbled cheek. He ran his hand under the back of her long-sleeved blouse.

They heard Mike coming and broke away. He carried the cat. He took two beers from the refrigerator and offered one to Duncan.

"Thanks," Duncan said. "Look at the size of those arms. Are you on somebody's team?"

"Nah. Not now. I played football in high school and did some wrestling."

"Yeah? Me too. Let's see what you've got." Duncan took off his glasses, set the beer down, and crouched in a menacing attack stance.

Mike grinned and put the cat on the table. They grabbed each other's arm and tucked their heads onto each other's shoulder. Sarah lifted herself to the counter and cheered for one, then the other. Duncan caught Mike behind the knee and pushed him into the table, scudding it noisily against the oven. The cat jumped onto the stovetop and then leaped out of the room. Mike and Duncan fell to the floor. Their legs locked together, and Mike rolled Duncan over on his stomach. Duncan grimaced as his head was pressed to the linoleum, but he heaved and threw Mike off. He got behind Mike, clinched his legs around his waist, gripped him in a choke hold with one arm, and with the other he bent back his leg. One of Duncan's shoes came off. "Say, 'Chicken knuckles,'" Duncan said.

Mike twisted and bit Duncan's arm, easing Duncan's grip. He spun away and pinned him to the floor, his knee in Duncan's back.

"I give up," Duncan said. "That's enough." He got up. "You're mean, boy. Like wet oak in a thunderstorm."

"You think I'm good, huh?"

Duncan rubbed at the tooth marks on his forearm. "Your brother's a wild one," he said to Sarah. "Get him a helmet."

Mike beat his chest and grinned. Sarah slipped off the counter and handed Duncan his beer. "You're both insane," she said.

"Let's have a look at these folders," Duncan said.

Mike left calling for the cat.

Sarah got up early the next morning and packed an overnight bag. She had told Mike she had business out of town for a few days. At work, Duncan was in meetings all morning, and she kept busy at her desk filling out forms and making calls. Everyone there worked in one large room that was sectioned into eight glassed-in cubicles. Occasionally, she turned around and watched Duncan talking to clients or taking notes with the silver pen she had given him. Whenever she caught his eye, he kept a straight face and went back to whatever he was doing. No raising his eyebrows, no sticking out his tongue, no A-O.K. sign or lip pucker.

He went out to lunch without her, which was normal since both wanted to avoid suspicion. Sarah usually brought something to eat in her purse and ate in the office. She was eating grapes, putting the seeds on a yellow paper towel, when one of her coworkers sat down in the chair in front of her desk. She offered Sarah a slice of chocolate cake. Sarah took it and placed it by her pencil cup, wishing she could eat it.

The woman's name was Doris, and Sarah didn't like her very much. She wore tight skirts and too much jewelry, making clients, Sarah thought, feel uncomfortable. Sarah always wore loose dresses that she considered sensible. She had only five dresses, anyway, and Duncan discouraged women from wearing pants at work.

Doris unwrapped her own slice of cake, licking chocolate icing off her fingers. "I guess you heard about Duncan's wife," she said. "I knew she was desperate for attention, but that's ridiculous, don't you think?"

"I'm not sure I understand," Sarah said.

"You know, honey. Duncan's a bit of a maniac."

Sarah took a grape seed from her mouth and tried to sound gossipy. "But I didn't know his marriage was shaky."

"I'm surprised to hear you say that."

Sarah stared at the wheat crackers in her plastic lunch dish. "What are we talking about exactly?"

"We're discussing Duncan, sweetheart."

"Maybe you should talk to yourself," Sarah said.

Doris polished off the cake and balled up the chocolate-stained cellophane it had been in. "I guess I'd better get back to my desk," she said. "You know, I used to think you could use more makeup. But what the hell, you're young. You need something else entirely."

Sarah watched her leave and threw the cake in the trash can. I don't need this, she thought.

Duncan came in from lunch with his jacket thrown over his shoulder. He called Sarah to his office. She had to walk by Doris on the way, but Doris was on the phone and just looked up at Sarah and smiled. Duncan closed the door and sat down at his desk, twirling the silver ballpoint.

"Is Doris looking this way?" Sarah asked.

He peered over her shoulder and shook his head.

"I've got some bad news," he said. "Barbara's back."

Sarah didn't say anything. There was a sliver of grape peel stuck between her back teeth and she touched it with her tongue.

"She can get around pretty well on her crutches," he said. "And she wanted to come back home."

"That means you can't see me tonight?"

"I'm as disappointed as you are."

"Right." She got up and went back to her desk. She looked at Duncan, who hadn't moved. When she felt she was going to cry, she snatched her purse and left as fast as she could.

Driving home, she got on the causeway and tried to blow up the engine of the Festiva. Then the steering wheel started to shake, and she slowed down. Every few minutes she pounded the dashboard and cursed. She drove dangerously, swerving in and out of the passing lane, even after she exited. She screeched into her apartment complex and stormed into her apartment.

Mike lay on the sofa with his feet on the wall, drinking a beer and watching a soap opera.

"What's the matter, Sis?" he said.

"Get your stinking feet off the wall. And get that ugly cat out of here." She went to her bedroom and cried.

Mike followed her. She lay across the bed clutching the spread in her fists. He sat beside her and placed his hand on her back.

"What happened, Sis? You get fired?"

She reached for a tissue and blew her nose.

"They canned you for sounding like a hog?"

"Shut up, Mike," she said, and buried her face in her arms.

"Of course, I'll kill whoever hurt you," he said. "Somebody break your heart?"

She sat up and dried her face on his shirttail. "Am I just spoiled or is the world out to get me?"

"You're spoiled, Sis. Who else has me?"

"Mike, you're as stupid as hell."

"But I discovered I can cook." He went into the kitchen and brought back a lopsided chocolate cake. She started crying again.

"Touching, isn't it?" he said. "I learned how just for you."

"Go away, Mike. I just want to be alone, O.K.?" She lay down again at the opposite end of the bed.

Mike put the cake on the night table. "Sis?" he said.

She didn't answer.

"Can I tie you into a knot?"

THE STORY
OF ART HISTORY

Tony had some time to kill before seeing his friends. He preferred to wait until he was sure they were home before taking the bus ride over there. He had gone to the university library but it was closed, and after the two-story library at the junior college where he worked, he had looked forward to the six floors of books where, during the years he had lived in this town, he used to fantasize for hours about sudden romance among the stacks.

Instead, only a talent show audition in the auditorium offered anything of interest. Tony had wandered in and seen a skinny boy doing the Pop. The boy, in a big white gangster hat, suddenly slid magically backward across the stage on one foot. As Tony walked along the yellow curb that stretched winding to the exit gate of the campus, he stopped and hopped backward, hoping to skate all the way back to the auditorium. He couldn't do it.

At the gate there was a rush of traffic in front of the campus. Four dump trucks loaded with gravel crowded the two-lane street, roaring in high gears in front of a line of closely following cars. When the traffic ceased, Tony was approached by a bum, a tall man with dignified posture. He wore a lint-covered cardigan and a checkered sports coat, and his frayed green shirt was buttoned only at the neck.

"Pardon me, young man," the man said. "What time does it get dark in this town?"

"Shouldn't be too long, now," Tony said.

"I see. Is there a Salvation Army?"

"I don't know where it is. Downtown is that way about three miles."

The man hadn't shaved in several days. He faced Tony, his legs crossed stiffly, and rubbed at a patch of blond beard near his chin, looking elegant and irritated. "I've got blisters on my feet this big," he said, showing Tony the size of his thumb. "Look at that."

"A bus comes along every half hour. Forty cents, it used to be."

The man uncrossed his legs and reached in the pocket of his too-short brown pants, pulling out fifteen cents. He held the coins in the center of his deeply creased palm.

Tony clinked a quarter on top of the change. "Too bad about your feet," he said. "It's not a bad walk."

He trotted to the other side of the street, thinking it was curious that he was called "young man." The bum didn't look much older than he, only taller. He wondered whether the man was really dignified. He headed toward the intersection and considered picking up the twelve-by-fourteen photograph of his grandmother which his aunt was having framed, but the frame shop was in the opposite direction from any of his friends. It would be something to do tomorrow.

At the corner, he noticed that the brick tobacco warehouse that had been ripped out last year was now the promised mall. A few cleanly dressed women were leaving the building, coming down the wide steps, putting on sunglasses. He went to the tall door of the mall and found it breezy there. The space inside seemed vacuous. The mall had been designed to preserve the open, rustic look of the warehouse, rough wooden beams bracing the wide corridor walls and supporting a curving, airy staircase that rose gently from the left side of the brick floor.

Most of the glassed-in rooms were not yet leased. Some still contained workbenches and rolled carpets, with large strips of tape crisscrossed on the windows. He passed a small newsstand that was in service, where a man in a shiny tan suit ate an ice cream cone and talked with the blushing clerk. Beside the newsstand was a shop that sold colorful silk-flower arrangements. Tony entered an import store.

He noticed first the rows of green saucer-shaped lamps hanging from the high ceiling. The ceiling was made of narrow planks of wood, like the floor of a backyard sun deck, and bright Peruvian rugs hung over the railing of the balcony that traced the top of the room. Several people were browsing in the store, though no one seemed to buy anything. They lingered among displays of stained glass bowls and plates, or showed each other the jade vases.

Tony passed a smooth mahogany elephant in the middle

of a pile of fancy pillows, and went to the glass jewelry counter across the room. Two pretty girls who were there moved away. He looked at earrings dangling on a revolving rack, and put one with tiny blue stones to his ear, looking at himself in the oval mirror on the counter. He thought he didn't look young at all. He had lost a lot of hair. He thought he'd be glad to see Doug, with whom he used to talk late at night about astronomy. He smiled to himself in the mirror, for practice at first, and then, around the eyes, he glimpsed a family resemblance.

Behind the counter, a tall young woman with a wide gold wedding band and short orange hair said the earrings were very lovely.

"Yes. I can see that," Tony said.

She stared at him with narrowed eyes, and smiled weakly as if thinking of something besides earrings.

"They're not expensive," she said. "They're handmade by a wonderful woman in the mountains."

Tony placed the earring back on the rack. "What about those bracelets?" Tony asked, pointing to the counter. "Who made them?"

"I'm not sure." She stooped, slid open the counter door, and placed the black tray of silver bracelets on the counter-top.

"They make a nice gift," she said.

He touched a couple of the bracelets without moving them. When he looked up the woman was staring at him again.

"Yes?" he said.

"Didn't you used to sell vegetables?"

"No," he said, as a teenage girl in pink ribbons pulled her mother to look at the bracelets. He turned and walked to a large straw basket full of paper umbrellas. He took one out and opened it. It was tan with bamboo sprockets and a green zigzag-striped pattern. A man in a white, short-sleeved Polo shirt gripped Tony's elbow. "Will you come with me, please?" the man said.

"What for?"

"For a moment."

Tony closed the umbrella and put it back in the basket. They went to a small office where the jewelry counter clerk sat waiting for them in a bentwood rocker. She had large calves.

"That's him," she said.

"Mrs. Joyce, here, believes you might have taken some jewelry from her counter without paying for it," the man said.

"Who are you?"

"I own the store. Clinton Wells."

"I'm Tony Ramsey. How's business, Clinton?"

"Forgive my having to ask, but empty your pockets on the desk, Mr. Ramsey."

Tony looked at the man, and at the woman. "I'm not getting along well, am I?" he said.

"Please, Mr. Ramsey."

He pulled out some money, his wallet, and a key, and laid them on the green felt desk cover.

"Is that everything?"

Tony dug in his left pants pocket and pulled out a nub of a carrot.

"Okay," the man said. He glanced at Mrs. Joyce and
arched his eyebrows. "We apologize for the inconve-
nience," he said to Tony. "Let me suggest that, if you don't
plan to purchase anything, maybe it would be best if you
left the store now."

Tony gathered his things and left the office, the store,
and the mall.

Outside the sun was setting, turning the sky yellow and
magenta. He walked about half a mile and saw the street
lights blink on. This was the first time he had caught that.
He stopped at a tavern run by recent college graduates, a
place he had gone to now and again before he left town.
Loud reggae music was playing through speakers mounted
on thick plywood platforms above the inside picnic tables.
One of the men working there recognized him and gave
him a free Michelob. That was odd to Tony because he
had never really talked with anyone there. The man told
him how he had just had to kick out a guy who was asking
everyone for a ride downtown. Tony drank the beer and
played a space game.

When he left, the sky was dark. He got on the bus and
thought about the bum awhile. He got off a block from
Doug's house, a brick structure built in the forties, located
across from a fire station. The last Tony had heard, Doug
had married a French girl who needed to get married so
she could stay in America. At the reception Doug had
pissed on the floor when the manager asked them to leave
the hotel. Tony wished he had been there to maybe fall in
love with the French girl. He walked the block thinking
that yellow curbs looked better under streetlights than in
sunlight.

Tony knocked on the door.

"It's open," Doug said.

He found Doug lying on the floor in a sleeping bag with a sleepy-eyed, long-haired girl. Doug sat up and laughed.

"Tony. When did you hit town?" he said. "How the hell are you?"

"Fine. Fine. Nice night."

"Man, are you bald. You know that?" He introduced Tony to Jane.

"I've heard a lot about you," she said. "You look good." She didn't sound like a French girl.

Tony sat on the striped couch to the side of Doug and Jane. They were watching a televised movie of a very short José Ferrer as Toulouse-Lautrec. Empty cartons of Chinese food were scattered around them.

"How many months have you been camping here, Doug?"

"About three, right, Jane?"

Jane giggled.

"I can't blame you for staying put."

"Are you hungry?" Doug asked. "I was just going out to get some food."

"Sure."

Doug got up and put on the pants that were draped over a chair. "So, are you a good teacher?"

"Not really. My students don't believe what I say."

"Yeah? Well, you've got that kind of face." Doug put on a jacket and zipped it up. Jane got out of the bag, wearing a short T-shirt and red bikini panties, and walked into a back room.

"I'll soon return," Doug said.

He went out the door and Tony relaxed, scanning the plaster walls. They were decorated with front pages of the *New York Post* and posters advertising past art exhibits.

Jane came back wearing white shorts.

"Am I mute?" she said.

"What?"

"I've been calling you from in there."

Tony could see the red panties through her shorts. He crossed his legs. "Those posters are yours, right?"

"Right. That's what I was calling you for. I'm majoring in art history, see. And I've got this incomplete that needs taking care of so I won't have it hanging over me all summer."

"I teach physical science."

"I know, but you're a teacher, right? And you know what teachers want. Help." She grabbed her hair and began twisting it into a knot.

"How old are you?"

"Seventeen," she said. "I'm smart." She put a bobby pin between her teeth and smiled at him, a dimple appearing in her plump right cheek.

"What do you have to do?"

She leaned over and placed her hands on his shoulders. Her hair fell from its knot. "Great," she said. "In the bedroom." The bobby pin dropped on his chest.

They went into the room where five handwritten pages were lined up on the bed. She knelt by the bed and handed him the first page. "I'm stuck," she said.

Tony knelt beside her and read. It was a rambling,

grammatically correct essay proposing that Paul Gauguin was evil, and using his painting as proof.

"Okay," Tony said. "You're stuck because you haven't defined evil."

"Everybody knows already." She put her hands on his thigh and twisted her mouth.

"I don't want to deal with this. I don't know a thing about art history." He got up and walked around the bed. "I saw some earrings today that would be perfect for you."

"You've got some bad in you," she said. "You like to do bad things, don't you?"

"Don't be stupid. How long should Doug be gone?"

"He's probably waiting for a pizza to cook. You can't take criticism. Can you take a joke?" She stood and turned her back to him, reading the pages.

"Do you have more than one pair of red panties?" Tony asked.

She looked over her shoulder at him. Then she went to the dresser and pulled open the top drawer. "See?" Tony walked over, stumbling slightly over a lump in the linoleum. The drawer was full of red lingerie.

"Red really sings," she said.

She took off her shorts and the T-shirt, and put on a long gown with thin lace down the front. She twirled for him.

"I haven't had much fun," he said.

"Doug loves this stuff," she said, lifting the garments from the drawer and letting them fall to the floor. "Take off your shoes."

Tony watched her for a while with his arms folded. He

scratched his neck and then sat on the bed and removed his shoes. He thought he heard something at the window behind the bed, but when he turned to look, nothing was there.

"And your socks, too," she said. "Feels terrific."

She continued dropping clothes until the drawer was empty and the floor between the bed and the dresser was covered with red nylon and lace.

"Stand in it," she said, stepping up and down in place and smiling. She shook back her hair and reached for him.

Tony rolled his socks and stuffed them in one of his shoes. He walked into the cool, limp pile of red and wiggled his toes.

"Slippery, isn't it?" Jane said. She was bouncing now.

Tony kicked up a camisole and caught it. The flimsy material against the linoleum floor let him slide his feet far apart from each other, and back again. He started sliding himself backward, not quite as prettily as the boy in the auditorium, but with relative ease all the same. "Do this," he said to Jane, and Jane did it. She let out a little scream, clutching his arm and stopping off balance. He thought she screamed from delight. She was smiling, but with her free hand she pointed to the window where Tony could see the face of the bum ducking away.

"What was that?" she said.

"It's okay," Tony said. "I know him."

"Yeah, but what is he?"

Tony shrugged. "Come on, let's dance." They went on sliding about. They did a lot of spinning, getting their feet all bound, with Tony laughing and dizzy. Jane balanced herself with her hands on his hips, and slid herself out into a bridge.

Then they heard voices and footsteps very near. Doug appeared at the door holding two six-packs of beer, and the bum was behind him carrying a big square pizza box.

"What the hell are you doing?" Doug asked.

"I don't know," Tony said.

"Me either," Jane said. "You met Tony's friend."

"This guy?" Doug said. "I invited him. Jesus. Try and act respectable, you know?"

Doug and the man sat on the bed. Doug opened two beers and the bum opened the large box on his lap. The smell of hot pizza wafted in the air, and Jane held on to Tony's sweater as they slid around rumba-like. The bum tucked a sheet of Jane's essay into the front of his collar as a bib, and supported a heavy slice of pizza with both hands. As he bit, he peeped up at Tony and Jane.

"This is quite a pleasure," he said. "Quite a pleasure, indeed."

YARD LIGHTS,
WATER, AND WINK

Rudy has not changed as far as Alice can see. Rudy is always old. When Alice was little, Rudy was old. The silver Mercury is still sequined. Rudy is still a wizard.

Alice drives. Rudy sits in the back as always.

You learn anything at that school?

Yeah. I learned a few things.

You looking kinda pretty, girl. You're still making those pictures, ain't you?

Snatching spirits like a pro these days.

You can make some more of me if you want.

That's exactly what I want.

Alice remembers when she was eight. She ran in the night playing hide-and-seek, sweaty and short and excited. The yard lights shone in the clearing where children scrambled and parents sat fanning in short sleeves. She ran to a dark pine and saw him, a lighted cigarette in each nostril, fireflies stuck to his pants. He made Alice dream. No one in her family dreamed.

That night Alice dreamed of people with eyes all over their faces, people with four, five, six, arms and legs. Rudy told her that was usual. Your grandfather knew it but he didn't use it. Maybe you, maybe you will. You're a little girl dreaming of everybody at once.

At twelve she was asleep in her room with her cousin spending the night. Her father came in late and drunk with the family blue vodka on his breath. Doors slammed. Alice woke up. Who's the best cook? her daddy yelled. Who's the best goddamn cook? He shook their beds. Scramble some eggs. I'm as hungry as a hole in the sky.

Oh, Daddy, she said. I was dreaming a good dream.

Randolphs never dream, he said. No dreaming. He ruffled their braids. Ain't that right, Trudie? And he hollered, I'm hungry, then vanished.

Alice focuses on the road. It is Ritual Day. All of Alice's family will celebrate survival at her house. They will drink the blue vodka in communion. They will survive it and be happy and dance in counter-rhythms. Turtles and rabbits will stew in steel pots.

Alice drives Rudy to the barbershop. The jeweled Mercury Marquis feels strong. She works the power sunroof, power seats, and power windows. The sun sparkles and spectrums the stones on the hood.

I ain't no goddamn wizard, Rudy says.

Rudy never needs a haircut. He is always bald. Alice has always laughed with her father about it, and smiles as she thinks of laughing at home.

Well, you could have fooled me, Alice says. If you ain't a wizard, who is?

I know I could have fooled you, girl. I can fool anybody. Even myself on a good day, but this ain't a good day. I ain't had a good day in some time.

You haven't been feeling well?

It's nearing September, and it rains in September. That's a fact.

My roof leaks. It leaks on my face. Every year it makes me look different.

You look just the same.

I have forgot how I used to look. My face gets wet, it gets fluid. It runs down the drain when I wash it. One day it's gonna stay gone.

Alice glances at Rudy's face in the mirror. She has taken photographs of him with her Nikons. Her daddy gave them to her to wean her from dreams. Reality, he said. Study it. Rudy looks like a man. That is, he does not look like a boy. He looks past fifty, sixty, seventy maybe. His face is heavy and smooth. His nose is bulbous and waxy. He wears plaid shirts. He has had a heart attack. Died several times. The doctor said it is a miracle he survived. What's a miracle to a wizard? Alice thought. When Rudy left the hospital, the doctor said a ballooned spot remained in his heart as thin as a worn piece of inner tube. It could pop any minute, the doctor said. But Rudy is worried about his face.

Alice chuckles. Rudy, you're a wizard all right. What else could you be?

I could be down the drain. His look is wide and placid.

Well, you're a wizard, no doubt, then.

Rudy rubs his face. His fingers are thick, like candy bars. He smells of lime. An empty orange juice bottle rolls on the floor of the passenger side.

Your grandfather was a wizard, girl. We called him Engineer. He could do anything. Except he didn't do much more than make poison and keep your uncles out of trouble. Took a wizard to do that then as now, the way they're always beating crap out of some cracker gas station attendant or something. But poison was his pride. Something he left. Of course it ain't worth a damn except it kills thirst like a motherfucker. But I ain't got a thing, Aly. Except this here 'mobile. September is coming. I told your daddy, made it legal, when I'm gone this 'mobile is yours.

Alice keeps her eyes on the road, moving into downtown. Traffic. Lights turn green when she approaches, but she slows anyway. She frowns. Rudy has been old so long it has never occurred to her he worried about dying. Rudy makes pictures worth taking. He quick-smiles in duels with the flash, and wins. He sneaks winks onto prints hours after the shutter has closed. If Rudy dies, she thinks, her daddy will take over. Don't give the blue vodka to Rudy, he says. How about a zoom or tripod for Christmas?

Ain't it odd, Rudy says, how a cave can be dark for so long and be lit in an instant by the spark?

Alice looks in the mirror.

You want a little nip, Rudy? she asks.

You got a little nip, girl?

The Ritual is in progress when Alice gets home. Alice has silver beads in her hair.

Empty rum and bourbon bottles are on the wood block in the kitchen. Steam sifts from the top of steel pots.

No more rum? No bourbon? big aunts ask and laugh.

Alice's daddy towers. A giant. Holds the bottle of blue vodka in two fingers by its neck above his head. Then pours in low-held glasses. Its light blue the color of special Popsicles Alice loved as a child.

They drink and whoop. Light blue dribbles on the chins and chests.

An aunt bounces over to Alice. She wears gold lamé slippers and a black nylon wig. Alice, where have you been? My lord, you have grown. Getting as tall as your daddy. You've been riding old Rudy around, haven't you? That foolish old man. Stay away from that old drunk, girl. He'll want your liver.

Another aunt comes up in a houndstooth pantsuit. Don't tease the girl now. Alice, sweetheart, I'm so proud of you. Everybody is. Do all the girls at that school wear their hair like that? You poor motherless child. I know your daddy's glad you're home. You know you really ought not to spend so much time with Rudy when you get so little time with your family, girl.

Daddy, Alice says, slipping her hand on his waist.

What is it, baby? he says, turning to her. Where's your glass, sweetheart? He looks over the crowd of dancing relatives. Somebody get my baby a glass! he says. His teeth and tongue are blue.

Daddy, she says, pulling him into the hallway. Rudy's scared of the rain.

Rudy's old, honey.

I know, Daddy, but he's scared.

Her daddy swigs from the bottle.

He says he doesn't know how he looks, Daddy.

Well. He licks his lips. Rudy's old now.

I think he's going to die, maybe.

Rudy's old, baby. He puts his face down to hers. And dangerous. Now get yourself a glass. Go say hello to your cousins.

In a day Alice's daddy draws some money and has Rudy's roof fixed. Rudy is happy for weeks. He goes to see his girlfriends. He teases Alice about doing "that," making a fist with his thumb between his fingers. He sits in his house on a swivel chair. Your granddaddy and me were just like this, he says, spinning, joining two fingers toward the sky. Then he sucks down the vodka from a coffee cup and makes little high-pitched noises from his head.

Rudy wants a haircut. It is raining. He walks to the car under a black umbrella. He wants to see an old woman later. It is Sister Harland who lives in Croix with a red palm on a sign in her yard. Alice is driving. Her hair beads are silver and crystal. You want a barbecue sandwich? Rudy says. I can't stand a bald-headed female. Alice pictures Sister Harland, whose hair is gray and braided like the horns of a water buffalo. She pictures herself in horns. Now, says Rudy. My head's as nappy as a goat's ass. She looks in the mirror and smiles.

Alice focuses lights in the raindrops before the wiper wipes them away. She remembers times Rudy has nearly killed himself. Every autumn he sets his yard on fire and falls asleep on his front step while it burns. Her father calls for help. Flashing fire trucks scream into his driveway, waking him. Leaping firemen with hoses scatter the flames with water. The day before she left for school she took him to see Sister Harland. She waited in the car for an hour, watching the sky in the puddles on the lawn. An old man drove up and rushed inside with a gun. He stepped in the puddles. Alice rushed behind him and screamed. Rudy was in bed with the woman. He had his undershirt on. The gun clicked and fell harmlessly on the pillow where the old man threw it. Rudy dressed, talked, embraced the old man, and left on Alice's arm. Sister Harland clutched a quilt at the door and waved as they drove away. Alice's daddy had words with Rudy. Rudy said Alice was grown.

Alice watches the smear of the windshield. The windshield wipers are silent. The wet street is satin to her. Cars along the side are yo-yos. First she hears a rustling in the back, and then a swish of street. In the mirror Rudy has his hand on his chest. Alice turns her head around. His eyes are closed. His head is out the window.

The steering wheel seems to change shape in her hands. She pulls to the side of the road, and her feet are numb on the brake. For a while she sits and stares at him, her chin on the soft velvet back of the seat. She waits for the inevitable wink.

I DID THAT

I

I sat in the front yard near the street under the shading cedar trees, digging in the lawn with a spoon. It was summer, and the air hummed — I felt the slightest effervescence in the air, in the grass, in the dirt, in the spoon. I was a child, and the ditch made deeper by a hill rising to the road was like a moat of protection aiding my oblivion to the passing cars and bicycles.

While I sang to myself, my head bent and eyes fixed on the damage I was doing to the ground, my legs stretched before me and the white rubber heels of my red sneakers rubbing the green off the grass, I felt the spoon tremble in my fingers. Sunlight shimmered off it. And I became aware of the rumble. I looked up and saw the dogs running in the road. They were a pack of fierce, bristling fur. They ran at me at an angle from the top corner of the yard, bounding over the ditch, barking pink gums, white teeth, and black eyes and noses. I scrambled up to run, but my sneakers were new with too much room to grow in. I fell, sat up and levitated by the seat of my shorts. The dogs nipped at my elbow, but I was fast. I zoomed feet first on the fizzing air to the safety of the porch. The dogs veered off across the yard to the road again, their tails high.

"Dogs that bite you," I said several times that summer. I was otherwise too young to tell more.

II

I was five and wearing a blue seersucker short-pants jumper. Something was slowing my parents, so I was outside remembering not to get dirty. I lingered at the side of the house by the newly bloomed dogwood, blowing the heads off dandelions, blinking at the purple and yellow baby flowers in the grass. The dandelion heads burst and dispersed, bits seeming to flame in the sun, lifting suddenly and disappearing. That seemed like fun, so I stood erect, caught a breeze and surprised myself by rising up the length of the dogwood, viewing the light in its petals until I drifted over it, easy as I pleased. My father came out and called my name but I didn't answer. He walked round to the side of the house, lingered by the tree over which I hovered, called me again, and walked to the back to the swing set. I was a secret suspended in the springtime.

III

I began to confuse silence with invisibility. Not merely in the way schoolchildren sit mum in the back of a room, though my experiments with silence took that form. Sure enough, teachers did not call on me in class, kids did not speak to me or look at me during recess and lunch. I was convinced that I could disappear if I was silent. I would walk the most dangerous streets — skim them hushed. I discovered other invisibles, nearly invisibles really, since I could hear them. Others could not, I guessed because they were listening to something else, like their thoughts or their heart beating and so got mugged without ever knowing what hit them. But I could hear their shoelaces tap, the wind in their jackets, the in and out of their breathing. I moved among them, my shoelaces trimmed, my clothing fitted. Back then, I held my breath for hours.

IV

I saw color on the screen of our black-and-white television. Red shirts, blue eyes, tan vests, amber dust under the hooves of horses. I sat there until I knew the color of things. Days of the week had color then. I don't remember them all now. Thursday was blue, still is, I suppose. Tuesday was brown. Wednesday, I believe, was orange. Saturday was gold, I think. And later, when I was fourteen, flashes of powder blue, small as a feather, would herald something pleasant — like the fair or a visit from an uncle in a new green car. Sometimes the flash was lavender. Now it is violet, though I don't attend long enough to welcome the pleasure, if indeed there is any pleasure. But the color still darts before me now and then, across the steering wheel of my car, out of the glove box as I search for a pencil, from the pages of a book. I notice women wearing it spread on their eyelids. Magic approximated. They disappoint me. I met a woman who told me that her eyelids were naturally blue. Whatever.

I once went blind in the dorm room of a charismatic basketball star. A bank loan gotten on the strength of his being a first-round pick resulted in a Lincoln Town Car, a quadraphonic stereo system, and a pound of ganja. I passed the face mask to someone sitting next to me in the circle, and watched a whirl grow from the periphery of my eyes until I sat in the dark, or perhaps oblivious to the light. Later, when I had been ushered outside, the thin outline of the world appeared in bright cobalt blue. It was Thursday.

V

I fell in love when I was six years old. My parents held my hand as we walked up the street on our way to my first neighborhood picnic. When we got to the top of the dirt road that led to the picnic grounds, I saw a beautiful little girl standing about sixty yards away with her parents and some older children. I had never seen her before. I had never before been down that dirt road. It was sheer discovery. I broke from my parents and ran full speed toward her, and would have run into her had her father not caught me. I had wanted only to touch her; she had the softest-seeming skin. My father, fearing that I would fall on the rocks, trotted up behind me and laughed something to her parents. I learned that we would be in first grade together. Through the years, I always loved her, and no one has ever caused me such longing and questioning of fate. I have been in love with others since I developed the pride and intelligence to quit trying to make her love me. But those other loves have been like the adding on of blankets. No matter how many cover me, it is the first one I always feel.

VI

When I was twelve, I dreamed of falling in a hole. It was a monumental shock. In the dream, several of my friends and I were running through a construction site, skirting a deep, bulldozed crater. I fell, and while I was falling, I thought, it's me. I had always been awed by the fate of boys who drowned during an unsupervised race across a river, who were shot with a neighbor father's gun, the boy whose branch broke, or who was bitten by the Rocky Mountain tick. The dream was the first inkling that I could be that boy. At the peak of an adult depression I parked inside the gates of a rock quarry and walked to a hole so large that I couldn't imagine it was real. I severely wanted to fall. I felt immensely silent and insignificant. I held my breath, and when I put my heels to the edge and leaned back, I floated, just bobbing on the gray quarry air.

PIMP

What was I doing? I was painting my toenails red when Mrs. Bell came by with bags of Avon. I walked on my heels to the door. She was beaming. She told me that Todd was in town, and that I should get down to Aunt Jo's and hug him.

"I certainly will," I said. "Right away."

She put the bags on the coffee table and straightened her patent leather belt. As usual, her slip was hanging. Todd and I, in our childhood efforts to be helpful in her kindergarten, used to remind her with whispers of the nylon sagging beneath her hem.

"Well, hurry up," she said. "No telling how long he'll be here."

She told me to try the new perfume, tearing open the stapled top of one white bag, handing me the small bottle.

I thanked her and told her that Mama would pay for the Avon when she got home.

When Mrs. Bell left, I sat on the floor and blew on my toes. Opened issues of *Cosmospolitan* and *Ebony* were scattered around me. I had been reading articles on orgasm and entertainers in a self-conscious effort to gain some social sophistication for college. I couldn't remember when I had last thought about Todd. I hadn't seen or heard from him in over six years, when, I felt, he abandoned me. I was thirteen then and he was fourteen, the year he moved with his parents to Minneapolis. I used to dream about him, and write him letters about what happened at school and what I found in the woods. Mostly I found the knives and spoons he and I would swipe from our kitchens and bury near pine trees as time capsules.

When he had been gone a year, and I had written him some twenty-odd letters, I heard the local rumor that he was a pimp and had a Cadillac. I didn't even know what a pimp was.

I asked my mother, and after staring at me awhile, she said it was an illegal job. My father said I should forget about Todd. I was embarrassed to ask anybody else. The other girls never talked about Todd. The neighborhood boys, from whom I had heard the rumor, behaved as if I should already know. Finally, I got out my dictionary. I was surprised to find the word in there.

I wondered how one went about being a pimp. I wrote to Todd and asked him, but he didn't answer that letter either. Eventually, I gave up on it. I stopped hanging out in the woods so much. I made the cheerleading squad.

When I got to Aunt Jo's house (Todd and I used to pretend we were cousins), Todd opened the door. He was big, with a barrel chest, and hands that reminded me of baseball gloves. He had the same smile and squinting dark eyes that I thought must have been great assets to his business. He wore a short-sleeved safari shirt, unbuttoned to the waist and the shirttail out. His normally light skin was almost orange from sun. I held open my arms and he hugged me so tightly and warmly that I cried right there on the doorstep.

"Becky," he whispered in my ear. "You feel wonderful."

He stepped back, holding my hands in his. His hands felt as soft as pillows. "And you are lovely," he said.

I wiped my eyes and laughed. "You look damn beautiful yourself." I reached up and kissed his cheek, soft and moist, and smelling of lime-scented after-shave.

I asked, "Where's Aunt Jo?"

"At the grocery store. How've you been, Becky? Come on in and talk to me."

We sat on Aunt Jo's pale yellow couch. I perched on the edge, turned toward him. He slumped back with his legs crossed, his ankle propped on his knee.

He said he was leaving in a day or two. He had arrived by train. He was going to buy a car and drive cross-country.

"I thought you had a Cadillac."

He chuckled, obviously laughing at me. "I had two. But I had to get rid of them."

I waited for him to say more. He just looked at me, his smile gradually fading.

"Well, congratulate me," I said. "I graduated last month."

"Aunt Jo told me. You're going to college and every-thing."

"Yeah. Duke."

"That's great. You want some lemonade?"

He got up and walked into the kitchen. I went behind him and watched as he poured from a pink plastic pitcher into blue plastic glasses. We sat at the kitchen table and drank.

"I guess you're not a pimp anymore."

He shook his head and licked a bit of lemon pulp from his top lip. "I've been a pimp, a bouncer, a bodyguard. Until yesterday I was a lifeguard. That's how I got this black." He held out an arm to admire.

"Hero work."

"Just staying out of trouble," he said. "And forget about that pimp stuff. I was horrible at it. The first girl who chose me turned out to be a man."

"Huh?" I frowned over the glass I held to my mouth.

"I was set up. I was at a club, and these other guys put this beautiful drag onto me. She asked me to dance and was being real affectionate when Fish, another pimp, got upset and started claiming she's his. It was a chance for me. I said, 'Let the girl choose.' She cursed Fish out and left with me. I heard all the laughter, laughing at Fish, I figured. We went to my place. I had a room. Well, anyway, I did better eventually, but it was too much bother, really."

"But you were only fifteen."

"Right. That was the best part. Then when I was sixteen

the woman I was living with got pregnant. Suddenly, she didn't like my nightlife. One day after the kid was born she shot me in the thigh. That stopped my nightlife for a while, and it also stopped my living with her. Then, that started a bunch of judges hounding me for child support. I spent three weeks in jail rather than give her any money, until Daddy heard about it and sent her a thousand dollars."

To me, this was like reading, something that was real until you pulled back and looked at the pretty cover, the author's name, and knew what was in the book couldn't harm you. And Todd was a pretty cover, leaning back in his chair, his big clean hands gently holding the plastic glass.

And Todd was harmless. I remembered the Halloween night when he faked his own hanging. A bunch of us kids were making our way through the woods behind his house after finding that he wasn't home. His mother didn't know where he was; she had thought he was with us. One of the older boys was lighting the path with a flashlight. We discovered Todd hanging from a thick rope tied to a tree limb. We stopped in our tracks. I remember screaming. Then Todd burst out laughing, kicking his feet. I didn't understand. But I loved him for it. For being all right. It was the best Halloween.

"What are you smiling about?" he asked.

"You." I reached over and touched his arm.

"Thanks for writing to me. I didn't write back. I didn't know how to talk like I still lived here."

I nodded. "So what do you have? A boy or a girl?"

"A little man," he said.

We heard Aunt Jo at the door, and Todd got up to let her in. When they came into the kitchen, I was standing, and Todd carried two bags of groceries. Aunt Jo and I chattered about how good it was to see him, how we wished he would stay longer. Todd opened a beer from one of the bags and said we could come with him if we wanted.

"Boy, I'm not going anywhere with you. No telling when you'll bring me back home."

"I'll bring you home, Aunt Jo."

Aunt Jo laughed and shook her head. Her hair was long and black, like a girl's, unlike my new short style chosen to make me look older. She asked if I would stay for dinner. But I had to go home and cook.

I walked home along the gravel shoulder, cutting through Mrs. Bell's yard where her patch of untended gladioli bloomed the color of grapes. I picked a few of the flowers, and looking up at her house, I waved to Mrs. Bell's plump brown face, which had appeared behind the glass of her storm door. She clapped her hands together, applauding me, and I waved again, brandishing the long, fluttering stems.

I got things on the stove and in the oven, and I watched the news on the little TV in the kitchen. I creamed the potatoes while "Family Feud" was on, not believing the all-female family from Texas. Asked to name a state famous for tobacco, the girl with hair to her waist said, "Washington, D.C." I cringed, embarrassed for her at first, and then just plain disgusted.

"Stupid," I shouted.

My father came through the door as I said it.

"My students on television?"

He plopped his vinyl briefcase on the counter and stared at the set. The woman's relatives were telling her what a good answer that was. Daddy imitated a game show host. "Name a weapon used by black street gangs."

"Atomic bombs," I said.

He buzzed me.

"Nerve gas."

He buzzed me again.

"Semiautomatic night-scope blowtorches."

"Bing."

He turned down the volume and looked in the copper pots. "I'm going to take a shower," he said.

I turned the sound up again and went back to the potatoes. I had the table set and all the pots on warm by the time Mama got home from the adult reading class she taught. The flowers were in a vase as a centerpiece. She peeped in the kitchen and smiled. I put the food on the table.

We ate to "Jeopardy." I told them Todd was back, that he seemed O.K. and looked really well.

"How long is he here for?" my mother asked.

"Not long."

"Good," Daddy said.

I looked at their faces. Neither of them was smiling. So I made jokes about how big he had gotten. By the time I finished telling them what I knew of his plans, they were thinking of him as a little boy again.

"You tell him he'd better not leave before coming around to see us," Mama said.

"He wouldn't do that, Mama."

Daddy rinsed his plate in the sink.

I waited up watching Johnny Carson, thinking Todd should have called or come by. Mama and Daddy were in bed. When Carson began thanking his guests, I pushed the off button on the remote control and sat listening to the silence, wondering where Todd was. Then I heard a car in the driveway. With the television off, no light was in the room except the weak illumination from Mrs. Bell's gas lamp in her yard next door. I looked out the window and saw a dark, gleaming, wedge-shaped car with its parking lights on.

I slipped on my rubber thongs and went quietly out the door. The night was warm, almost like no temperature at all. The only coolness I felt was the dew on the grass as I traipsed through the yard to the car. I loved our yard at night. There was always a slight haze, and the big trees seemed as soft as velvet.

"Hi," I said.

Todd was sitting there with the radio on. "You like it?"

"I guess. Hard to tell."

He opened the passenger door, and I went around the front and got in. The dashboard was a wide blue glow. The upholstery was blue tweed.

"It's a Chevy."

"Let's go," I said.

We drove around listening to a jazz station. Todd

passed me the beer he had been holding between his legs. I took a sip and settled in. "How'd you get it so fast?"

"Know-how."

"License? Insurance?"

"Yep."

"Are you sure?"

"I'm thinking about shaving my head."

"I don't think so, Todd. Your face is orange and your scalp would be white. You'd look like a snowcapped pumpkin."

"Shit."

I sipped from the beer again and offered it back. Todd wore a navy blue sports coat over the safari shirt, and blue jeans. I looked at my legs stretched out before me, thin and brown up to my terry cloth shorts. I pulled at the cuff at my thigh.

"It's dangerous to dress like that," Todd said.

"Mama buys these things. They're comfortable."

"Your mama wants you to walk around like that?"

"I guess. It's the little girl look."

"I like it. Where to?"

"I'm just not ready to go home."

The digital clock on the dashboard read 12:45. The town was quiet, and Todd maneuvered the streets as if he were familiar with the loops and one-way avenues that now characterized the city. Once, just before Todd's family packed up and moved, when his parents were out of town scouting new residences, Todd and I took his father's Plymouth for a ride. I was amazed then that he drove so well, that he knew streets I had never traveled. Todd had a crush on a majorette at another school and we drove to her house. I stayed in the car, glad to be still, fearing getting caught by police on the ride home. Todd walked to the back of the house looking for the girl's bedroom window. He returned angry, his face tight. We roared out of her driveway and ran stop signs and red lights. I was too terrified of everything to speak. We never did see a policeman.

Remembering that, I now felt safe with Todd, not only because of the charm that seemed to protect him, but also because of the distance from him that I felt. I didn't really know him, now. Whatever touched him couldn't touch me.

We were downtown by the big bank building where his father used to work. I was never sure what his father did there, but whenever I imagine him I see him in a suit and tie. He was a mild man, as mild as my own father. He became active in civil rights and lost his job. It was soon after that he moved his family away.

"You know what I've always wanted to do?" Todd asked. "Lasso that bank, hitch the rope to the back of a tank, and drag it on its belly down the street."

I closed my eyes, listening to the music, luxuriating in the new smell of the car, feeling as if I were floating on a carpet through the night. Todd drove straight. I fell asleep.

When I awoke, we were at a truck stop. The clock read 2:52. Todd was getting out, and when he saw my eyes open, he said, "Gotta pee." I watched him go into the bright diner where several men sat slumped at the counter. He hesitated, looking around, and then disappeared off to the left.

I got out. There was a line of tractor trailers parked about fifty yards from the building, and a couple were at the gas pumps farther to the right. I went into the diner to find out where we were. Just as I got inside, a man got up from a booth and blocked me.

"Hey, slut," he said.

He cradled a tan cat in his left arm. He wore a sweatshirt with the sleeves cut out, and dirty army pants. He pointed to my crotch. "How's that doing?"

I glanced over at the counter waitress, who was serving what looked like two plates of gravy to a couple of men in jean jackets. "Where am I?" I asked.

"Ouch," the man said. "Didn't I tell you not to do that?" He held the cat with both hands over his head, revealing the thin white deodorant ring under his arms. The cat dangled, its legs stiff and claws extended.

Todd came out of the men's room hitching his pants to smooth his shirt. "Hi," he said to me.

"You like pussy, fella?"

Todd broke his smile to look at the man, who held the cat out to Todd.

"Don't put that cat on me." The anger on Todd's face was unnerving, more chilling than the baby-faced anger at his sweetheart's house years ago.

"What you scared of? Everybody likes my pussy." The man pushed the cat closer to Todd.

"I believe you heard me," Todd said.

The men in the jean jackets swiveled around on their stools. They were laughing. Todd's eyes were narrowed, his shoulders tensed, and I was shivering in the air conditioning.

The man stuck out his tongue and hugged the cat again. Todd took my elbow and led me back to the car.

"Where the hell are we, Todd?"

He started the engine. "Don't *ever* leave the car with the key in the ignition," he said.

"What's going on here? Look at the time. I'm supposed to be home, man."

He put his arm across the back of the seat and turned toward me. His hand rested behind my neck. "You wanted to ride, didn't you?"

"Come on, Todd."

He sighed and looked annoyed. "What do you have to be home for? You ain't got a job to get up for. You got anything to do tomorrow?"

"What are you, crazy?"

"Sure I am. Aren't you?"

I studied him hard to see if he was.

"This is not fun." I faced the diner. The man with the cat paced back and forth in front of the counter, his head bent to the cat's ear, his lips moving.

"Becky, it's all right," Todd said. "I want to see Charleston, that's all. And I want you to see it with me."

"What? We're in South Carolina?"

"Almost. You want to call home?"

"I want to *go* home."

Todd touched my hair, and I flicked his hand away. He frowned and touched my hair again. "Don't want to go home," he said. "Want to be with me."

"This is not working. This is pretty dumb."

"Is it? Look, we'll just drive. We'll find a place to sleep

and you can think of what to say. In the morning you can
call home and say it."

"Goddamnit, Todd."

He put the car in gear and headed for the highway. I
folded my arms and held my legs close together. I felt
scared and stupid, as if I had stepped out of the house
without any clothes on and the door had slammed shut
and locked. Todd drove slowly, without talking. He
ran up the window to close out the noise of the transfer
trucks that passed us. Finally, he lit a cigarette. I turned
up the static on the radio and searched the dial for a
station.

"Do you remember the spider that wrote your name in
its web?" he said. "You actually believed you had seen
that."

I didn't know what he was talking about.

"You were seven," he said. "You thought you were
going to die. Somebody told you it meant death. I told you
it wasn't important."

"Is this a trick?"

"No, it's very clear to me. You were not in danger then
and you are not in danger now. We're friends, aren't we?
You love me, don't you?" He cracked his window and
blew smoke out.

I struggled to control my voice. I enunciated carefully.
"I don't appreciate any of this."

"No kidding," he said.

We got off the highway and hit an old country road. A
sign said Swallowsville was twelve miles away. The clock
showed 3:37. I watched twelve minutes blink away until

we approached the town, its advent announced by re-
duced–speed limit signs.

No one was about. We passed a Holiday Inn and a
Sleepy Time Motel. At the bottom of the hill was Hotel
Lloyd, its name printed vertically on its side. A yellow
neon VACANCY sign shone in the lobby window.

Hotel Lloyd had a small lobby with dizzying brown,
geometric-patterned carpeting. The clerk sat behind a
glassed-in booth that was exactly like a movie theater ticket
window. His clock radio was tuned to a talk show.

Todd tapped on the window with his knuckles and
spoke through the round metal grille. The man stood and
slid a registration form through the semicircle opening.
The corner of his left eye was blood-red.

"We need a room with two beds," Todd said, handing
the man a credit card.

The man pointed to a chained pen on the counter. Todd
filled out the form quickly, and the man took down a key
from the cork board above the radio.

"Elevator's over yonder," he said.

The elevator door was already open. Todd punched the
third-floor button. "Trust me," he said.

"Right."

When we got there, I walked off ahead of Todd as if I
knew where I was going. "This way," Todd said. And I
followed him to 327.

The hallway and the room had the same dizzying carpet. The beds were covered with gold, fake-velvet spreads.

"Not too bad," Todd said, turning on the air conditioning.

The room smelled like a basement. The lampshades were crooked, and the one on the stand between the two beds had dark stains on it, as if water-damaged.

"Are you thirsty?"

"I don't care."

He went out, taking the key with him. The telephone didn't even have a dial. I looked in the mirror and brushed my hand over my hair. I fiddled with the television and found "Leave It to Beaver." I left the volume down, and then got under the covers of the bed across from the set. I got up to turn off the air conditioning, but that made the room too quiet, so I turned it on again. In the drawer of the lampstand there was a Bible, a Hotel Lloyd notepad, and an eraserless pencil. With the pencil, I shaded the top page of the notepad to see what the previous occupant had written. Nothing showed up.

Todd re-entered noisily, pushing open the door with his foot, his arms loaded with soft drink cans, the room key dangling from his finger. He set the drinks around the lamp. I had the covers pulled up to my neck. He popped the top on a Diet Sprite and drank long from the can.

"Whew," he said, and pointed to the others. "Take your choice."

There must have been eight cans grouped there, all cold and sweating. Keeping the bedspread tucked under my chin, I reached for a Coke. Todd grabbed it from me and opened it, then gave it back. He sat on the bed, by my knees.

"Have you thought of what to do?"

"I'm going to shoot you in the ass."

He laughed. "I must look like a target."

"You act like an idiot. Like you want to get killed. Daddy is going to kill you, if I don't."

He leapt onto the other bed. "What's he gonna kill me with, his briefcase?"

"Go to hell, Todd." I tried to drink the Coke and spilled some down my chin, onto my neck.

"I'm not an idiot," he said. "I know what I'm doing, even if nobody else does." He pulled off his shoes without unlacing them and stretched out on the bed, balancing his Sprite on his chest. He still wore the sports coat.

"Everything I've done has been with you in mind," he said.

"You forgot about me, Todd. And I forgot about you. So what is your problem?"

There was a silence. Then he said, "Aunt Jo told me you had your pick of colleges. Why'd you choose Duke?"

"Who cares?"

"You were afraid to go far from home. You were afraid to leave your mama and daddy. You were afraid I'd come back and you would be nowhere around."

"What am I afraid of now?"

"Don't you know that I need you? You're no dummy." He sat up and finished off the soda. "You know that car is stolen," he went on. "Now you pretend that I'm stealing you, too. Well, call the cops and get a free ride home. You can even tell them where to shoot me."

He lay down again and closed his eyes, his fingers laced over his belt. I shifted to my side, propped up on my elbow.

"What do you have in mind? Let's see," I said. "We'll

leave the Chevy near some country used car place. There'll be a lot full of dusty Buicks and Datsuns, with their prices in broad white paint on the windshields. There'll be one with RUNS GOOD painted across the front. We'll buy it, or steal it, and head south stopping at McDonald's to eat Happy Meals. We'll check out New Orleans, sleep in dumps like this, and grill Steak-umms on a hot plate."

"We can do better than that," he mumbled. "We'll go to class reunions and eat shrimp."

"Do you have *any* money?"

"I can get us that car. And I can get you some clothes."

I went to the bathroom. When I came out, Todd was in the same position, his eyes still closed, all laid out like a dead man. The stubble of beard was visible on his cheeks.

"I told Mama you'd come by and see her before you left."

"I haven't been seen in years."

I grew angry all over again, for his not being seen in years, for creating a situation that would worry everyone, for his wanting me to decide his fate. I sat up against the headboard and bit my thumbnail. I spit out what I tore off with my teeth. I picked up my Coke and hurled it at him. It made a metallic pop as it bounced off the side of his forehead.

He covered his face with his hands and turned over toward the wall, his back to me, his legs curled under him. He didn't say anything and he didn't move anymore.

I swung my legs over the side of the bed. "Todd," I yelled, but I was afraid to yell too loudly. I tiptoed over to him and peered down. His mouth was drawn to a grimace.

There wasn't any blood. I touched his shoulder and he jerked. "O.K.," I said.

I slipped back under the covers and stared at the ceiling. Water from somewhere, perhaps the bathroom upstairs, had left a large stain in the shape of a bell. That made me think of Mrs. Bell, asleep, floating in her bathtub and spilling out in a flood of scented bubble bath. I thought that when the morning news came on TV, or when the morning grew light, I would call my parents. I imagined their surprised, relieved, strained voices. I heard them spitting Todd's name, and myself saying that it wasn't important.

When I woke up, I called and told them just that. Todd was gone.

MONROE'S
WEDDING

Thompson sat on the tractor mower and watched Monroe blow leaves up against the chain-link fence. The sun had nearly set; the sky was a luminous purple and red. They were working on the grounds of the graphics plant, which sat high on a hill. Even from the bottom of the slope where Monroe assaulted the air, one could look down on the freeway a mile away. Thompson knew that Monroe was just tired, not actually stupid. But he looked stupid now. It would take them another hour to pull the leaves out of the links by hand.

Monroe started up the hill toward Thompson, carelessly exploding a raked pile before turning off the blower. It was cold, and wind raced through the power lines that streaked the sunset. But Monroe had been working on his feet, with a motor strapped to his back, clearing a hundred-by-thirty-yard area of a full season's worth of fallen leaves.

He had taken off his jacket and gloves, and now approached Thompson in a sweatshirt bearing the name of a college he had never attended. "Hey," Monroe called. "I gotta tell you something."

Thompson let him make it all the way to the mower before responding. He kept the vacuum-attachment motor running because of the trouble it took to start it. "What is it?" Thompson said.

"Well. It's like this. I'm getting married. I want you to be the best man."

Thompson stared down at Monroe for a while before chuckling and shaking his head.

"It's you or some joker I can bribe," Monroe said.

"You can't bribe me?" Thompson said.

"You're the best man I know. Besides, you do the paying, remember?"

"Not for headaches."

"It won't take twenty minutes."

"The fence, I mean."

Monroe looked down the hill. He breathed into his hands and rubbed them together. "Creative landscaping, I call it," he said. "I like it."

The next day it rained, but Thompson met Monroe early for breakfast, as was usual during the three weeks Monroe had worked for him. Monroe lived in the Crescent Motel, a place used by truckers and construction workers during the week and by people seeking inexpensive privacy on weekends. It was on a highway stretch of car dealerships and discount stores, and surrounded by a high iron fence overgrown with vines. Monroe had lived there for two months, since moving from Kentucky to find work in construction. When nothing turned up, he answered Thompson's newspaper ad. His room was on the second level, facing the pool, but Thompson preferred waiting for him in the restaurant off the motel lobby.

The morning waitresses were students from the black state college — Thompson's alma mater of fifteen years. They were attractive young women for the most part, and sometimes he would tease them about their grades, plead for extra bacon. He'd ask about their boyfriends as a way to get intimate. Then he'd ask if they liked children — still thinking about affection, but mostly imagining them as babysitters for his two daughters, who had moved to Alabama with their mother. Next he'd bring out the pictures, and know he'd blown it. He didn't really care. He figured he missed his girls more than he missed romance.

That morning he didn't joke with the waitress who brought over the pot of coffee and cups. He was thinking about how the rain would put him behind on the bank branch he kept up. One of the national vice presidents was to visit the next Friday, and the manager wanted the grounds extra neat. Thompson unzipped his down-filled vest and unbuttoned the collar of his shirt. If the rain slackened, he'd at least clean the gutters. Monroe could take the day off.

Monroe sauntered in and joined Thompson in the booth by the window. He pulled his work gloves from his back pocket and laid them on the table next to the sugar rack.

"Boss," Monroe said, "I'm wearing two pair of pants. How many you wearing?"

"We're not going out today. Which is good for you, 'cause you got a marriage to plan."

"I'll live happily ever after. How's that for a plan? You going to be my best man?"

"I guess. If you're serious. When's the wedding, anyway?"

"Sunday after tomorrow. You got a suit?"

"A gray one. I suppose you want a gift, too."

"We need a vacuum cleaner. What's a good kind?"

"I have a round, flat thing that floats."

"Futuristic. Something like that you could get us."

"How about a plate?" Thompson said.

"A plate's O.K. Whatever."

Thompson laughed. "How will you spend this free day?"

"Do I ask you that?"

"No."

"All right, then."

Thompson poured coffee into their cups. "May I ask whom you are marrying?"

"Carol Dunn, that's whom," Monroe said. "She knows you."

Thompson wondered how that could be. He had been a track star in college, and had his picture in the paper as recently as four years ago when he was inducted into the local Sports Hall of Fame. But he doubted if any woman Monroe's age, which was twenty, knew about those things. Of course, his name was printed on magnetic signs on the sides of his truck, but most likely Carol Dunn was the daughter of somebody who remembered his heyday.

"I'm a public figure," Thompson said.

The waitress came to take their orders. She was majoring in mass communications and wore glasses with her initials etched in a corner of one lens. Monroe asked for corned beef hash and scrambled eggs, and Thompson wanted a steak biscuit. She asked if they wanted something sweet.

"Shame on you," Thompson said. "We're practically married men."

After breakfast, Monroe went back to his room and Thompson went home to his duplex apartment on the other side of town. The rain didn't let up, so Thompson sat on his green Barcalounger and assembled a new Weed Eater while watching "Donahue" on television. Thompson had a town-house maintenance contract in a planned housing community, and Monroe referred to the women they saw on the tennis courts there as Donahue wives — wives who didn't have to work. Thompson's own wife was a hard worker; he had to give her that. She had been a runner, too, and long after Thompson had given up the sport she continued to rise at four in the morning to put in three neighborhood miles before cooking breakfast and going off to haul sandwiches and snacks for a catering and vending-machine company. The thought of Monroe's upcoming marriage caused Thompson to miss his wife, to wish he were still married. She'd had the chance to advance in her company if they moved, and he was starting up his own business where people knew him. He had just gotten the big loan to buy equipment. They argued, and she got chummier with her manager, and Thompson got jealous. Within what seemed like no time at all, she decided that the perfect solution was to take the promotion and transfer to Mobile. She and their daughters had been gone seven months.

Thompson's TV began to sizzle. He looked up from the Weed Eater to see a thin, white string of smoke rise from the back of the set and spiral into oblivion. The room held the smell of electric burn. What would the Donahue women do now? he wondered. He decided to take the television to the shop, which would give him a chance to get his suit to the cleaner's and maybe find Monroe's gift.

The dry cleaner had a drive-up window, and a man in a diamond-patterned sweater said Thompson's suit would be ready on Monday. The repair shop promised to call later with an estimate. So Thompson drove to the mall near his apartment. His intention was to browse Fran's Gifts for ideas for Monroe and his bride, but signs on the rent-to-own store attracted him. They offered easy acquisition of the store's merchandise — painless payments and no credit checks.

There was a mock living room full of striped furniture at the front of the store, and some white washers and dryers lined the right wall. The left wall held three rows of VCRs atop various-sized television sets. A woman smoking a cigarette sat in a glass booth in the back. Thompson scanned the TVs — half of which were tuned

to "The New Price Is Right" and the others to a soap
opera. The sound was turned down on all of them, and
Thompson couldn't decide whether Bob Barker's tie was
supposed to be green or blue.

A woman came out and asked how she could help him.
She was short and fairly plump, and wore boots and a
corduroy dress. Voluptuous, Thompson thought. Her hair
was light blond and very fine, revealing a flushed spot at
the crown, where a thin curl turned the wrong way.

"My television is on the blink. It sizzles," Thompson
said.

"These don't sizzle," the woman said. "And these here
can be had for just twelve dollars a week." She waved at a
group on the middle shelf.

Thompson bent and stared at the screens. The soap
opera showed a young couple dancing together in a large
studio. The man was dressed in a black tank top and black
tights. The woman wore a leotard that was either green or
blue. During a close-up, they seemed about to kiss, and
Thompson looked away. He noticed the saleswoman's cigarette, still burning in an ashtray on her desk behind the
glass.

"What's the best picture?" Thompson asked. "Look.
What color are her eyes?" The couple were now kissing,
and though the man's eyes were closed, the woman gazed
at him with astonishment.

"What color do you prefer?"

"Yours, actually," Thompson said.

"That would be this one. The green eyes." She tapped
the top of one of the sets. "It's remote, too."

The camera shot widened to include another young woman standing in the door of the studio. She wore jeans and a sweater, and clutched schoolbooks to her chest.

"That's the end of that," the saleslady said.

"Yeah." Thompson looked over to a rack of black stereo equipment in the fake living room. The dials were lit in orange.

"You want it?"

"For twelve dollars, yes. I only need it for a week."

"There's a two-week minimum. Plus a week's rent deposit. That's thirty-six dollars I'll need today."

"That's not what your sign says."

"Oh, that's only a sign. It's still a good deal. Come on back, so I can get some information."

She went into the glass booth and motioned for Thompson to go around to the other side, where there was an open counter with two barstools. She stubbed out her cigarette and brought a form on a clipboard up to the counter. Thompson gave her his name, address, and phone number, and told her where he worked.

"What do people call you?" she asked.

"What?"

"On the street."

He thought of names like Slick, Stretch, and Popeye, none of which people called him.

"Thompson," he said.

Then she asked for the names and phone numbers of three people who knew him. The only number that he could remember was Monroe's. He gave her that, and the names of two men who had been on his shift at the trucking company before it went bankrupt. He'd see them at the barbershop sometimes. They knew he had a business. He wouldn't give the names of clients, or of anybody connected with his track fame, or of anybody he had known with his wife.

The lady went back to her desk, lit another cigarette, and opened her phone book.

"They're probably at work," Thompson said.

She puffed on the cigarette and smiled.

No one answered the first two calls. On the third, she reached Monroe. She asked if he could verify Thompson's information. Then she laughed and said, "I don't know."

"What was funny?" Thompson asked after she hung up.

"He asked are you *renting* his gift."

"Oh. He's getting married. I'm the best man."

"Congratulations." She brought the form back and showed Thompson where to sign. "I trust you," she said. "I'll call the other two later."

"Would you like to go to the wedding?"

She laughed again, in a less spirited way than before. "That's crazy. I don't know either of you."

"You know us better than we know you."

"True. I cry at weddings."

"I might cry myself."

She pulled a Polaroid camera from under the counter. "Smile," she said, as she snapped Thompson's picture.

Thompson blinked, and smiled too late. A man wearing a windbreaker with "Pete" printed on the breast pocket pushed a dolly into the store. The lady fanned the photograph and looked at it. "It's almost you," she said.

The man stood the dolly beside Thompson. "What's up?" he said.

"I've just been arrested," Thompson said.

"Not yet," the lady said. "Pete, Thompson here has a TV that needs to go out." She handed Thompson the picture and came out of the booth to show Pete the right television. Thompson's picture looked the same as usual — stone-faced, his head held too high, his Adam's apple too big.

She returned to take the photograph from Thompson and staple it to the form. "I need the money in cash," she said. "Your next payment in two weeks."

Thompson gave her the money and led Pete to his truck. Then he trotted to the gift shop and bought Monroe an ironstone tureen.

The following week, Thompson and Monroe worked a few private lawns, the bank, and the town houses. Each day, Monroe grew more excited about his coming marriage. Tuesday, Thompson learned about Carol Dunn, the bride. She drove a truck for the catering firm that his wife worked for. Monroe had met her at one of the motel vending machines, and she had met Thompson at a company picnic. Thompson still didn't remember her, but he remembered those picnics. His wife would inevitably say something to embarrass him. He could not be completely upset with her, since she'd be boasting about him. But what she said was personal and exaggerated — like her comment to a group of women about his stamina in bed being as good as his stamina on the track. He wondered whether Carol Dunn had been in that group.

By Wednesday, Monroe had moved to the honeymoon suite. At breakfast, he told Thompson about the round, revolving bed and its red satin cover. He also described his suit, which was powder blue and had shoes and a tie to match. The wedding would be in the auditorium of Thompson's alma mater, with a reception to follow at the student union.

"I'm going to *give* the garter to you," Monroe said. "If she's wearing one. Some tender lovelies will be there."

"I might bring a date," Thompson said.

"If you can find one, right? That would be taking baloney to a banquet, believe me."

"What about the rehearsal?"

"No need. It's just me, you, and Carol and her buddy. And the preacher, of course."

"Monroe, why didn't you tell me before that you were in love?"

"The same reason you didn't say you were miserable."

Janine, their waitress that morning, brought the check to the table.

"You want to go with me to a wedding?" Thompson asked her.

"I'm too young," she said.

Thursday, they got the bank ready for the vice president's visit — spreading pine straw around the azaleas, edging up along the walkways, mowing one more time for good measure. Friday, they worked the town houses in the planned community. They were early enough to watch children going to school and husbands leaving for work. Around nine, the Donahue wives were on the streets — walking the younger children to the day care center and driving new cars to the shopping malls or the tennis courts. The very idea of their leisure made Thompson feel responsible for Monroe. He'd have to win more bids, enlarge his business, to make sure that Monroe earned enough to supplement his wife's income. And what if she became pregnant? He wanted to tell Monroe that getting married was stupid.

But he didn't. He filled his push mower with gas while Monroe pulled the season's last weeds from the shrubbery patch just inside the gate to the complex. He thought about the saleslady at the rent-to-own store, imagining how her life differed from that of a Donahue woman. Her family probably owned the store and considered blacks to be people who would steal their VCRs. But certainly she worked. He was fairly sure he could get her to go to the wedding with him; their encounter had crossed over the line between customer and salesperson.

He started the mower and guided it along the square of grass in front of the model town house. It was his newest mower — self-propelled — and steering it felt good and almost effortless. He was beginning to think about the wedding. He imagined his date as the only white person there, feeling out of place, scared she'd do something to offend somebody. Maybe she couldn't quite stifle a laugh when the ceremony turned out to be onstage. Or maybe she'd gasp when the bride entered wearing red. Maybe she'd wisecrack to the wrong person about the cake being shaped like a piano, or a peacock, or a truck. And Thompson would stand next to her — that incredibly white woman wearing pink wool — and not mind the crowd's attention at all. He would slip his hand around her waist and feel her stiffen slightly — sense her being eager to leave. And he would be amused, because this was Monroe's wedding, and this anxious, discomforted woman was not his wife.